# NO WAY OUT

## A JIM BRANNIGAN THRILLER

PAUL RAFFERTY

SQUINTER PRODUCTIONS

First Published in 2022 by Squinter Productions

Copyright @ Paul Rafferty 2022

The right of Paul Rafferty to be identified as the author of this work has been asserted by him in accordance with the Copyright, Design and Patents Act 1988.

*All characters and events in this publication, other than those clearly in the public domain, are fictitious and any resemblance to real persons, living or dead, is purely coincidental.*

ISBN: 9798363197031

All rights reserved. No part of this publication may be reproduced, stored in a retrieval system, or transmitted, in any form, or by any means (electronic, mechanical, photocopying, recording or otherwise) without the prior written permission of the author, nor be otherwise circulated in any form of binding or cover other than that in which it is published and without a similar condition including this condition being imposed on the subsequent purchaser.

A CIP catalogue record for this book is available from the British Library

*To My Children; Jack, Morgan and Madison*

*"May the bonds of Family last a lifetime"*

# Preface

*Jim Brannigan may be fictional but the organisations he encounters and their methods of operation are all too real. The satellite systems, surveillance techniques, the secrecy and the manipulation of world events are equally real and just as disturbing. Jim Brannigan lives in our modern world of subversive counter terrorism, lucrative political ambitions and the proliferation of fake news.*

*I was inspired to write No Way Out, my debut novel, after witnessing the constant bickering and fighting of our political leaders in the build up to the referendum on whether or not the UK should leave the EU. My research since then has been thorough, and accurate.*

*I have mixed fact with fiction to create an exciting political thriller grounded heavily in reality no matter how unbelievable it seems. The story you are about to read pulls together true crime threads from across the globe, draws upon the sins of the superpowers, and makes clear that any of us can fall victim to their whims in the pursuit of power. By the final chapter you won't take the news for granted any longer, especially if it comes from 'Government Sources'.*

*Thank you for choosing to read my book and please leave a review on Amazon.*

*"Everybody lies, every day, every hour...."*

**Mark Twain**

## Day One: The Set-Up
## Chapter One

Michael Logan's head throbbed as he woke to yet another hangover. He was used to the dryness in his mouth and the taste of sick at the back of his throat but he hoped that today would be a good day.

He rubbed his head slowly and let out a low moan, smacked his lips together in the hope of generating a little spittle and attempted to get up before crashing back down onto the busted sofa.

Battered furniture lay scattered around the room and a heady mixture of dirty clothes, empty beer bottles and food cartons cover most surfaces, including the floor. A faded photo of Michael and three smiling buddies in combat fatigues stood discarded on a dusty fireplace propped up by some old boxing trophies.

He reached into the pocket of his shirt, pulled out a crumpled piece of paper and squinted at it:

*Vanderbilt Building, 22b, Mercury Park, 3 pm*

John and Michael Logan stood at a crowded bar, John is Michael's older brother by a few years and is a successful lawyer. He was clean-shaven and well dressed; Michael was unshaven and looked like a rough sleeper. The music was loud and John was shouting. "I'm not giving you any more money Michael."

"After all I've done for you," replied Michael.
"Don't start with all that again, it was a long time ago. We were kids for Christ sake!"

"Yea, we were, but you needed your wee brother to look out for you, didn't you mister big shot lawyer."

"Christ! Here we go! You beat up the Flaherty brothers to save me from a kicking, then you had to run away to join the army to escape jail...Mom and Dad never loved you and it's all my fault."

"Good, I'm glad you admit it. Look, I just need fifty quid to tide me over. I'm working for an old buddy tonight. I'll pay you back. It's only a lousy fifty fucking quid! Your God-damn tie cost more than that for fuck sake! Come on, don't make me beg!"

"I'm not lending you any more money, Michael. But I tell you what; I'll give you fifty quid if you'll do something for me?"

"Anything big brother, you know me."

"It's David's birthday tomorrow and Marcy had booked a clown to entertain the kids but he's cried off sick so we need someone for an hour or so. I was thinking you could do your old magic act?"

"And the penny drops....that's why you wanted to see me....still needing my help BIG BROTHER after all these years. I guess my invite got lost in the post?"

"Look Michael, do you want the fifty quid or not?"

"No, if I'm to be the hired help I want a hundred. Union rates and all...and I want fifty up front."

John took his wallet out of his jacket pocket and handed Michael a fifty-pound note. "We've moved since you last visited. We're in the Vanderbilt Building over on Mercury Park, apartment 22b."

"I never visited you, John. You asked me to help you move into that wee apartment off Oxford Street about five years ago and I was never inside it since. David was around three at the time, I guess."

John ignored the jibe, wrote his address on a piece of paper and stuffed it into Michael's shirt pocket.
"Don't be late Michael. And for God's sake clean yourself up. You actually smell....do you know that?"

John walked off, leaving his brother at the bar.

Michael managed to struggle off the sofa and grab his old magic box from under the bed. He threw water in his face and brushed his wet hands through his hair. He stared at himself in the old mirror above the basin and dried his hands on his shirt. He sniffed the armpits and decided to go with it before slamming the door on the way out.

Although he was running late and he smelled, not that he noticed anymore, he figured a quick one on the way would steady the nerves, keep him focused and stop the tremors. Yea, they were getting worse but nothing he couldn't control. He was in charge, not the booze. Hell, he could quit any time, but why should he? He enjoyed a drink as much as the next man and besides, David was a little weasel, just like his dad, and for a hundred quid they were lucky to get him.

The Railway Arms was well lit, too well lit for Michael; it felt like someone had ripped a piece out of the sun and stuck it in the ceiling. But it was a good boozer with cheap drink and no trouble. Mark James had been the barman of the Railway Arms for as long as Michael could remember and he stood at the far end of the bar polishing glasses as Michael wandered in.
"What can I get ya Michael?"
"Whiskey."

"Whiskey! Bit early for the hard stuff, even for you my friend."
Mark set the whiskey and a small jug of water on the counter. Michael dumped a pile of coins beside them.
"Gee, thanks, MOM."

He swept the whiskey off the bar, scoffed at the sight of the water jug and sought refuge in the relative darkness of the small corridor beside the toilets. His hand shook as he sipped the whiskey. He stared at the glass before slapping it onto the table. The small corridor stank but Michael was only interested in his whiskey and the other fifty quid he would get from his stuck-up fool of a brother.

They were close once and although John was the elder it was Michael who took on the big brother role. He had been a stubborn child by nature and was always getting into trouble.

At eleven years of age he joined the local boxing club and by the time he was seventeen he had gotten himself a reputation, and nobody messed with Michael, inside or outside of the ring.

But they did mess with John and the day the three Flaherty brothers cornered him down the alleyway beside Speedy Muldoon's and gave him the beating of his life was the day that

Michael Logan could have spent the rest of his life in prison.

They said John had disrespected their sister by refusing to go on a date with her. John made it home with a busted face and two missing teeth and Michael flew into a rage. He bolted from the house, the screams of his parents ringing in his ears, and scoured the streets until he found the Flaherty brothers sitting on the swings in the kiddies' play park laughing. They stopped laughing when they saw Michael.

The police called to the house later that evening, Mr. Flaherty had made a complaint. His boys had been attacked in the park a few hours ago. Two of them were being kept in hospital overnight; one had a broken wrist and needed stitches to a gash in his forehead while the other still hadn't regained consciousness. He wanted Michael charged with Grievous Bodily Harm, but his boys weren't talking. Michael denied he had even been in the park but the police warned him that they weren't going to let the matter drop. They knew all about his reputation and that temper of his. The next day Michael quit school and joined the army.

He didn't see his brother for three years after that night and that was fifteen years ago. They had seen each other on and off since then, first when their father died, then their mum a couple of years later but they were never close again. John got a job 'in the City' that kept him busy 24/7 and Michael went to college once he got out of the army. Their lives drifted apart until Michael moved back into London and started hassling John for money.

His mind drifted back to last night as the whiskey started to work. The Goose and Hen was a lively bar; lots of people watching football on a big TV, Michael was sitting quietly in a corner scanning the bar when his mobile buzzed. A text message from John Carter: *Green sports jacket on his way, do not engage. Observe and report.*

All he had to do was go to the Goose & Hen pub on North End Road at 6.30 pm, watch the football and let John Carter know if a man in a green sports jacket met a woman in a blue dress. But that's not all that happened. Still, that would have to wait; there was David's party to get to and that fifty quid to collect. He gulped down the last of the whiskey and hurried out of the bar, reaching the bus stop just as the number 15 was pulling away. He almost fell in front of the damn thing causing the driver to brake hard and swear harder.

Michael lugged the magic box on board the bus and found an empty seat toward the back. The bus was slow to make its way through the lunchtime traffic and despite the bus filling up no one wanted to sit beside Michael.

Still, with no one to annoy him, he could concentrate on the party. He used to be good at this stuff as part of his college course at UCD he learned magic for a stage production of *The Magician's Tale* and then turned it into a lucrative sideline as *Mike the Magnificent*, Children's Entertainer. That was only a few years ago, before his mother's death, but as he struggled to remember it seemed to him that he was remembering someone else's life, another Michael Logan entirely.

At first, he barely noticed the woman sitting opposite him. Tall, dark complexion, late twenties, with deep blue eyes, quite pretty really but unfamiliar. Yet she seemed to be staring at him the way people do when they half recognise you but can't remember your name.

He had to get this party sorted, not start hallucinating about strangers on the bus. Maybe it was time to cut back on the booze and he smiled at the very idea of cutting back on the booze. Yet he couldn't shake off the feeling that this woman was watching him. His head hurt, and he couldn't think straight...what was she looking at? Michael glared at her until she got up and moved to the front of the bus.

She got off at the next stop and as she did so Michael was sure that she slipped what looked like a small bottle of perfume into the pocket of a well-dressed man in an expensive suit and Crombie overcoat.

The man moved slightly down the crowded bus to where he could now get a clear view of where Michael sat. He appeared to be idly scanning the back of the bus but Michael was sure that he was the focus of the man's attention. Maybe his paranoia was taking hold. Why would anyone be following him? The idea was so absurd that he dismissed it out of hand and let his mind drift back to the bar the night before.

The green sports jacket came in, ordered a beer and sat at the bar. Late forties, greying temples, distinguished looking but no one paid him much attention as City were playing and all eyes were on the plasma screen in the corner. A short time later the blue dress swept into the bar, Bombay Gin and a splash of tonic, pale complexion and wet, rose-red lips and City playing or not everyone noticed the blue dress.

She slipped into a seat at a little table beside the door. The green sports jacket joined her and soon they were in deep conversation. People drifted back to the game. Michael Logan was too far away to hear the conversation but he saw the green sports jacket hand the blue dress a piece of paper.

Jill Anderson looked blankly at the paper for a few seconds. "What am I looking at here, Ben? Hope this isn't what I gave up my face pack and prosecco for?"

"It's the referendum results for Clacton-On-Sea."

"Riveting, but what's your point? You said something about voter fraud."

"Look closer Jill, Clacton-On-Sea had a 70% turnout on voting day. That's 35,000 of the voting population who bothered to get off their backsides and vote. Now, look at the results: 17,795 voted to leave; 17,544 voted to remain and there were 36 spoiled votes."

"Yes Ben, very interesting but so what?"

"Because Jill, 17,795 plus 17,544 plus 36 equals 35,375."

"So, you're saying 375 votes were miscounted? That's more like cock-up than conspiracy."

"Yes, but I checked and the same thing happened in 52 out of the 382 voting areas and that's too many to be a coincidence."

"But who could do that? I mean who could be at every voting area to change the results if necessary?"

"Has to be the Local Counting Officer and they're appointed by central Government. I'm worried here Jill. Nobody knows about you, so you'll be safe. But someone sent me a folder containing referendum raw data. Someone wanted me to find out about the results and that puts me in danger. I need to go public on this, that's the only way I'm ever going to be safe. Can you get this to your Editor tonight?" He handed Jill a flash drive. Jill Anderson looks up to see two grey suits slip quietly into the bar.

"Jesus, NO!"

Two loud bangs and all hell broke loose. Michael instinctively dived under the table as people screamed in panic and confusion. He spun his head round to see the blue dress slumped in her chair, her head thrown back by the force of the Colt 44 bullet that entered through her right eye and exploded out the back of her head. Blood poured out of the wound in her face and down into her gaping mouth before dribbling down onto her dress and pooling on the floor below.

The grey suits were moving quickly now. One stood in the middle of the bar with his gun in his outstretched hand scanning the room for movement. No one moved and no one lifted their head. The other one grabbed the green sports jacket and coshed him with the butt of the colt, rendering him unconscious.

The blue dress was searched quickly and methodically and when the grey suit got to his feet Michael could see he had taken the flash drive from her lifeless grasp. The grey suits grabbed the green sports jacket under the arms, hoisted him off the floor and dragged him to the door of the bar. Then they were gone, just as the wail of police sirens filled the night air.

"Well, is this seat taken or not?"

Michael was snapped back to reality by the sound of a man's voice, raised and more than a little annoyed. The burly figure was already bearing down on him and without waiting for a reply he sat down, squashing Michael against the side of the bus.

Hungover, paranoid and now having the life squeezed out of him by a 250lbs monster in a hard hat and gloves was not the best start to a day he ever had. Still, he thought to himself, things can only get better...

As his stop finally approached, Michael stood up only to be grabbed by the wrist, "You drop this buddy?" said the monster in the hard hat and he thrust a folded £20 note into Michael's hand.

"Yea, must have," stammered Michael. "Thanks buddy".

He couldn't help but smile as he stepped off the bus, easiest twenty quid he ever made he thought to himself. Builder texted: *Package delivered.*

Michael was so pleased with himself and still hung over that he didn't notice the faint smell of scopolamine on the money as he shoved it into his pocket. He forgot all about the man in the expensive suit and Crombie overcoat, who was now following him through the afternoon crowd as he made his way along Harrington Road, crossing over at Nando's and then next right into Queen's Gate. Although he wasn't feeling so good now he put it down to the booze and last night's excitement. Still, he never had numbness in his hands and feet like this before. His legs felt heavy and he seemed to be almost pushing through the air in the street like he was pushing through clear molasses.

He was sweating and exhausted, his senses were dulled and the life around him seemed to be going on in slow motion.

Michael Logan stumbled along the street; he stopped to lean against a building and dropped his box. He stared at his right hand. It was red and swollen. He rubbed it and grimaced with the pain. "Scopolamine, shit!" he gasped.

Exhausted, he abandoned the magic box on the street and stumbled slowly forward towards the Vanderbilt Building, an imposing facade with wide steps leading up to a large mahogany door. John's apartment was on the second floor.

Michael staggered up the steps and managed to push the doorbell for apartment 22b. "John, they've poisoned me...Devils…Breath...John....do you hear me? John!" Michael waited anxiously for his brother to buzz him in. He was weak now, too weak to hear the footsteps behind him, too weak to react. As the buzzer sounded and Michael fell into the hallway and onto the floor his face was sprayed with scopolamine from what looked like a little perfume bottle and he found he could no longer move and he couldn't speak. But he was conscious, conscious enough anyway to recognise the Crombie Overcoat from the bus. Michael was lifted to his feet, guided to the lift, and up to Apartment 22b.

## Chapter Two

A flashing street sign hung outside the net-clad window plunging the room from dimly lit squalor into the complete emptiness of night. It was the only light the room had and all it served to show was the rancid dampness and dirt that survived in every corner. Pieces of old furniture were strewn across the floor discarded and left to rot, alone and in peace. This place was a shit hole.

Jim Brannigan stared blankly at the hooded corpse strapped into the only chair in the room. He hesitated for a moment, made a decision, and pulled off the hood. This man had been bound and gagged and left to his fate, a bullet in the head from a Glock 17. Brannigan didn't recognise the man but he kind of liked the green sports jacket he was wearing. This poor soul lay dead because Brannigan had been given a job to do.

He was ex-army, captain of his regiment, recruited for Special Ops then transferred to the Anti-Terrorist Unit, a new Government Department set up in the wake of 9-11 and the London bus bombings of 2005.

He was a field agent, not the spying kind but the killing kind. He was used to taking orders without question or hesitation and tonight was no different. His orders were simple, retrieve a flash drive from this man. If he didn't have the flash drive, kill him. If he did have the flash drive, kill him anyway. He didn't have the flash drive.

Brannigan turned and walked out of the room, closing the door quietly behind him. Someone would drop by later to clean up.

The wet grey night seemed to match his mood perfectly. He walked to the end of the near-deserted street and turned right. Walking past *Lazy Joes All You Can Eat American Diner* he noticed the photo on the TV screen inside the little café. It was a photo of the man he had just left on the hotel room floor. Underneath was the headline; 'Government Minister Missing'. Brannigan pushed open the door of the café and went inside. Low booths of red and cream leather skirted the room, black and white tiles covered the floor, and the main counter gleamed of chrome and white Formica surrounded by cherry red bar stools. The waitress was dressed in a rather short red and white striped dress with a matching cap, a red neck-scarf, and sparkling red shoes that looked like they had just come out of the Wizard of Oz completed the outfit. "What can I get you, honey?"

"Coffee, black, no sugar." said Brannigan. The waitress turned away, waving her hand towards the booths. "Coming right up. Sit anywhere you like. It's been a slow night." Brannigan walked to a booth in the far corner of the room and sat down.

"In other news," continued the television newsreader "*The Suicide bomber from last night's attack in London has been identified as Michel Logan, a one-time explosives expert believed to have been radicalised by Al Jahed terrorists while on tour in Iran with the British Army and now thought to be part of a sleeper cell working in Britain.*"

The waitress set the coffee down on the table. Brannigan hardly noticed as he continued watching the news. Images of the collapsed Vanderbilt building flashed up along with the picture of an old friend now plastered across the TV screen. "*It is believed the suicide bomber had strapped himself with explosives before entering a private dwelling and activating the bomb, killing everyone in the property, causing the world-famous Vanderbilt Building to collapse into rubble. It is believed the bomber's family were among those who died during the attack, but Police are not yet sure if they were involved in any way at this stage.*"

Brannigan left the café and crossed the road to make a call from the phone box on East River Street. "Susan it's me..... No, there was no flash drive..... Yes, it's done..... I know, Sir Alistair McIntyre, tomorrow morning, Café Mouton, Lower Harvard Street.....but there's something else, Michael's dead. Turn on your TV."

Jim Brannigan was connected to two of the biggest news stories in the UK and he knew that couldn't be a coincidence. Tomorrow morning, he had a meeting with Sir Alastair McIntyre, Director of ATU. He gave the orders and Brannigan wanted to get some answers.

## Day Two: Fake News

Brannigan ran across the road, narrowly avoided being knocked down by the oncoming traffic, and strolled down Lower Harvard Street, squeezed between a bookmaker and hairdressers. The street opened up into a courtyard, there was a small shop in the left-hand corner selling exclusive French coffee and little packets of sweet things at expensive prices. The courtyard was peppered with cast iron tables and chairs each one with a white parasol and covered with a white linen tablecloth. Ivy around the stone walls completed the look.

Sir Alistair was sitting in the far corner of the courtyard, his back against the wall. Impeccably dressed in an expensive suit, a black tie with red stripes, and sitting perfectly in the centre of a Windsor knot an emblem of a castle or a fort. It reminded Brannigan of a club or an old school tie perhaps but he didn't know which club McIntyre belonged to and he couldn't have cared less. Black Oxford brogue shoes completed the ensemble.

Brannigan sat down and glanced at the drink that was waiting for him, iced tea in a tall glass with crushed ice and a hint of lemon. He also glanced at the agents sitting at the other tables. Sir Alistair rolled his E-cigarette between his finger and thumb and smiled weakly.

"Didn't realise you'd organised a play date?" said Brannigan.
Sir Alistair scoffed. "You look awful dear boy. Not sleeping well? Job worries keeping you up at night?" he laughed lightly to himself. "Still, we're pleased with your work."

But Brannigan wasn't pleased; he wasn't pleased with the laughter and praise from McIntyre felt more like a kick in the stomach than a pat on the back. So he decided to ask the unspeakable question, "Why did Benjamin Rush have to die, and why torture him when you already had the flash drive?"

All pretence of a smile flickered and died on McIntyre's face "That is none of your concern." He spoke calmly and quietly but there was menace in his voice and rage in his eyes that Brannigan had not seen before.

Brannigan pressed on with another question "Has it anything to do with the explosion on Mercury Park yesterday?"

McIntyre remained impassive. "My, my, listen to you thinking out loud. You're an agent for the Anti-Terrorist Unit of her Majesty's Government. You're not the thinking kind of agent, you're the killing kind. I do the thinking, you do the killing. Understand? And besides, what do you care about Michael Logan? The man stole your wife away. What was her name? Jennifer, that's right Jennifer, and then he killed her in a drunken car accident. I thought you'd be happy. After all, that bomb did what you couldn't."

"And what was that exactly?"

"Kill the only man in this world you hate more than me."

"Oh, I wouldn't say that I hated Michael more than you."

Sir Alistair scoffed again and stared at Brannigan. "We're done here; you'd better go....while you still can."

Brannigan smiled. "But I didn't get a chance to play."

Sir Alistair looked around at his agents. "You wouldn't?"

Brannigan stood up quickly, the sudden movement shocked Sir Alistair and the agents tensed. "Oh I would, but I've to catch up with an old friend. Besides, this is a new shirt and I wouldn't want to get it dirty....not yet anyway. I've a feeling we'll get to finish this sometime real soon."

Brannigan left the drink untouched and made his way back out onto Lower Harvard Street. He opened the main door of his building and took the stairs to the third floor. He passed wee Jimmy Johnston playing in the hallway.

"Hiya, Mister Dillon."

"Hiya Billy, why are you not outside with the other kids?"

"Awk, I had another asthma attack last night and me Ma won't let me out. You know how she is when I'm sick, I can't leave the building, heck I can't even leave this hallway."

Mrs. Johnston had moved in next door about three years ago and little Billy usually played on his own every day after school. He was on some spectrum or other and was teased because of it. Mrs. Johnston never let him play outside. There was no sign of Mr. Johnston.

Brannigan got to his apartment door to find the lock broken. "Billy, do me a favour, go inside and ask your mum if we've had any visitors in the building today….and Billy"

"Yes, Mister Dillon?"

"Stay there till I come to get you."

"Sure thing Mister Dillon" Brannigan drew his Glock17 pistol from its holster and gently pushed the apartment door open.

The apartment was a mess. Everything was either upside down or broken. He stepped inside and moved swiftly and quietly, checking each room in turn. Satisfied that he was alone he looked around at the mayhem. There was a lot of damage, but it seemed to him that nothing was missing. He didn't keep anything of value in the apartment anyway. Everything had been bought from a house clearance sale and stood pretty much where the delivery men had left it.

He wasn't in the business of nest-building; this was somewhere he could leave in a hurry. It wasn't even in his name; well not his real name anyway, just one of the many aliases he had used over the years. He usually mixed his love of soccer with his love of music to create new identities; he had been Watford Lennon, Gunner Dillon, and his personal favourite Chelsea Jagger.

He got no answer from Carter's mobile, so he tried the landline, no answer there either.

"Hey Mister Dillon, me ma says....." Billy was standing at the door to Brannigan's apartment staring at the destruction.

"What did your mum say, Billy?

"Me ma says there was a man here earlier from the gas board checking for a gas leak."

"Didn't I tell you to stay inside Billy?"

"Yea but me ma said you'd want to know 'cause he was only interested in your apartment....what happened here, Mister Dillon?"

"I forgot to pay my cleaner Billy, now you run along. I have to go out."

At John Carter's apartment block Brannigan pushed each bell in turn on the wall beside the front door. The third bell from last he got an answer; "Hello?"

"Hi, I've flowers for Mrs. Bloomberg, apartment 22. She's not home and I wonder if you would mind buzzing me in so that I can leave them in the hall for her?"

"Sorry, can't do. No visitors allowed unless let in by residents."

"Listen, I get it but it's her birthday and these are from her daughter in Australia. If I can't get in I'll have to leave them here on the step and knowing London they won't be here when she gets back. It's up to you lady." The buzzer sounded and Brannigan entered the building.

The door of apartment 35A was opened by a tall slim woman in her late twenties; she had a dark almost Caribbean complexion and deep blue eyes.

She was wearing a blue and white striped dressing gown tightly wrapped around her shapely body. Her hair was ruffled yet her makeup looked fresh and her nails were painted.

"Where's Carter?" asked Brannigan, somewhat surprised to see a girl in John's apartment, never mind one quite so pretty.

"He's not in and who are you?" came the equally blunt reply.

"A friend," this woman was starting to annoy him.

"Jim Brannigan," she said it as more of a statement than a question, and when Brannigan didn't answer she nodded to herself and stepped back into the apartment. Brannigan followed. The main living room opened to a corridor on the right down which there was a bathroom and two bedrooms. On the left was a small annex for a kitchen and beyond that French doors that led to a balcony. The apartment was spotless.

Annette Chambers stood in the centre of the living room. "I'm Annette, John's girlfriend. I haven't seen John for a few days"

"How'd you know who I was?"

"John said if a rude man ever showed up looking for him and demanding answers it would probably be you."

"I phoned ahead but there was no answer."

"I unplugged the phone. I've been away for a few days and got back late last night. I didn't want anyone disturbing me until you come banging on the door." Annette Chambers paused for a second as though deciding whether or not to continue. "I am a little worried about John, to be honest, he didn't call me when I was away which is unusual, and he has been a little scared lately, not wanting to leave the apartment, that kind of thing".

Brannigan listened as Annette talked but there was something about her that was not quite right. Yes, he had noticed the flawless make-up, the manicured nails, and the rather concealing dressing gown but it was more than that. The John he knew loved mountain bikes and computer games. He must have had one hell of a makeover. There was nothing to be gained by staying there any longer and without Carter not much to go on.

"Well, If John contacts you tell him I need to speak to him," he said matter-of-factly and headed for the door.

"Wait! John said I should give you this if something happened to him." She picked up a piece of paper from the table and held it out.

"What makes you think something's happened to him?"

"Well…I don't know…. as I said, he hasn't been himself lately……now he's missing." Brannigan took the paper from her outstretched hand.

"Just one more thing, John Carter loved playing late-night sessions with people all over the world on Earth Invasion 3 or whatever the latest war game is these days but I don't see any signs of his computer. Now why would that be, do you think?"

"Maybe he just grew up....you should try it sometime."

Brannigan smiled and left the apartment. Outside, in the hallway, he looked at the piece of paper:

*McKenzie's Pawn Broker*
*Victoria Street*
*Ticket No: 080863*

McKenzie's looked like one of those family-run businesses that had been around forever and it showed; hidden down a side street, peeling paintwork and grimed-up windows that hadn't been cleaned since the rusted gridiron had been screwed in front of them. The stench of urine hung in the air all down the street and caught the back of the throat acting as a natural deterrent for anyone who thought of loitering there for too long.

The bell above the door sounded as Brannigan pushed hard and walked into the dimly lit shop. The counter was about five feet from the door and ran the length of the small shop. An iron grid, like the one on the windows, stretched from counter to ceiling creating an oppressive and rather claustrophobic little space. There was nowhere to sit so Brannigan stood.

A small man, no more than 5' 4", came out from behind a bead curtain and stared impassively at Brannigan. Brannigan placed the pawn ticket into the drop hatch in the counter and watched as the little man scooped it up and disappeared behind the curtain.

He returned a few minutes later with a small metal security box and a key. He placed these items into the drop box and waited. McKenzie's wasn't the type of place to offer privacy so standing in the small shop Brannigan opened the box, removed the receipt for a bus ticket that was lying in the bottom and thrust it into his pocket. He closed the box, put it back into the drop box and left. He hurried out of the side street to find some much-needed fresh air.

The bus station was a good 20-minute walk from Victoria Street, but it was a bright day and Brannigan needed thinking time. He had been surprised by the day's events, he was no closer to finding out what happened to Michael, although he was sure he was no suicide bomber. He hadn't a clue where Carter was, and he wondered what Annette Chambers was really doing in John's apartment. She was pretending for sure, and the pawn ticket was a little too convenient. Then there was his apartment. He was being played but he didn't know by whom or why so for the time being he had no option but to go along for the ride.

At the bus station he handed the receipt to the plump girl behind the glass in the ticket booth. She typed in the code on the receipt and handed Brannigan a one-way bus ticket to Edinburgh.

"Bit early for this one aren't ye darlin'? The train for Edinburgh doesn't leave till tomorrow morning. Guess you could always enjoy the sights and sounds of London...."

The girl's voice faded into the background. Brannigan tapped the ticket in his hand a few times then turned and walked away without saying a word while the girl was still talking.

"Well, I never, some people are so rude!" she said, but her protests were lost on Brannigan.

His accommodation options were somewhat limited; his place was trashed and although a hotel was a possibility he had a better idea. He returned to 35A to find Annette Chambers leaving. She looked surprised to see him.

"I was wondering if I could stay the night, and see if John turns up?" he said innocently.

She seemed somewhat anxious to get

away."Yea sure, I won't be home till tomorrow morning anyway. I'm staying with a girlfriend tonight, catching up on old times. If John turns up get him to call me" She turned to leave,

"Would you have a spare key perhaps?" asked Brannigan. "In case I got out for some food later maybe."

"Yea, there's one on the coffee table, help yourself"

She left, almost running down the stairs, banging the large front door of the apartment block behind her. Brannigan watched from the window in the hallway that overlooked the street to see her get into a black Mercedes 4x4 with tinted windows. He couldn't see the driver's face, but the window of the vehicle was down just enough on the driver's side for him to notice an expensive suit, a crisp white shirt, and a very distinctive tie; black with red stripes and sitting perfectly in the centre of the Windsor knot an emblem of a castle. Maybe it was another coincidence that the suit driving the black Mercedes had the same tie as McIntyre but then Brannigan didn't believe in coincidences and that made two in as many days.

He searched the apartment, working methodically through each room looking for anything that might give him some answers to his ever-growing list of questions, but the place was clean, orderly, and free from clutter, and that was the problem. The John Carter he knew wasn't a slob by any means, but he was a single man in his late thirties who wasn't given to spending his time cleaning. He loved the outdoors and his mountain bike and war games. Brannigan didn't care much for computer games or computers or technology for that matter. Too many ways to trace someone but he knew how to use them, he knew how to find people. But there was no computer in 35A.

**Chapter Three**

A few days earlier The Right Honourable Carol James MP sat in her office in Westminster gazing idly through the glass panel that separated her from her Junior Minister Benjamin Rush and through his office to all the other offices beyond. All stretching along a corridor, each one smaller than the previous, reflecting the importance of the occupant right to the very end, to the smallest office occupied by Mister or Misses Who Cares.

Her office was one of those huge wood-panelled affairs that ordinary members of the public never get to see. Hidden away behind armed police, bodyguards and bullet-proof glass it was so big it looked like a small library. She was Secretary of State for Exiting the European Union and she was smiling. The sort of smile a cat makes just after it gets the cream; she couldn't believe that everything was going to plan. Great Britain was leaving the EU as planned, Brexit was a done deal and the British people rejoiced. They couldn't see the bigger picture of course; they couldn't even imagine the bigger picture and she smiled again even wider than before. She pushed the intercom on her desk. "Benjamin, would you come in here for a moment, please."

Her Junior Minister was an intelligent, hardworking and diligent man. He had no family anyone knew of and his main interest outside of work was golf. He cut quite a figure around Westminster, whether representing the Government wearing one of his Savile Row suits or that trademark green golfing jacket he wore when a less formal approach was required. He got things done and didn't ask too many questions. He was ambitious and wanted a seat at the big table; the Cabinet. In his quieter moments he even dreamed that maybe one day he'd get the top job. He thought Prime Minister Rush had a certain ring to it.

"Now Benjamin everything is going to plan and we are finally leaving the EU in a few months but there are a few problems that need sorting. The BBC is focusing too much on the difficulties Brexit might cause ordinary families and protest marches are taking place across the county demanding a new referendum and we have to put a stop to it. We need to get rid of the Director General of the BBC, and when I say 'we' of course I mean you. Any ideas?"

"We could leave a briefcase on a train containing damaging information about the Director General being linked to that tax avoidance scheme in the Cayman Islands; mix it in with a few celebrities we all know are cheating the tax man for that extra touch of authenticity?"

"Excellent, a nice bit of fake news wrapped up in a blanket of truth. I like it!" replied Carol James. "Also, get another story out about the benefits of Brexit. You know the sort of thing; pick some squalid little hamlet full of migrants and the unemployed and show them how wonderful their lives are going to be post-EU membership. We need people to believe Brexit is good for them and that we are actually interested in making their lives better! Get the idea?"

"Yes Ma'am"

"I know I can rely on you Benjamin. You don't gossip over the coffee machine and you never break confidence; not even when you find a Cabinet Minister in a rather compromising position with a prostitute in the Speaker's Chair. Oh, I know all about that one, how do you think I got this job in the first place!" Carol James laughed and turned and stared out of her window towards Big Ben and London beyond.

"And Benjamin."

"Yes, Ma'am?"

"Don't wear that hideous green jacket in here again"

"Yes, Ma'am."

Carol James didn't look at Benjamin again and he knew the meeting was over.

There are fifteen government departments and Benjamin Rush worked as a Junior Minister in quite a few of them during the previous parliament. Some of the Ministers he liked and some he didn't, but he kept his opinions to himself. He was seen as a safe pair of hands; a solid chap who could be relied upon to do the right thing and put his country's interests above his own.

He also worked hard as a Member of Parliament for his constituents. As a sitting MP he lobbied for more money and resources to fight social deprivation, he openly supported David Cameron's Same-Sex Marriage Bill and he was credited with helping the Conservative Party end thirteen years of Labour rule. It was fair to say that Benjamin Rush was well-liked both in Westminster and in his own constituency.

He had known his new boss for only a little while, but he reckoned she seemed fair and considerate if a little distant and abrupt.
The smear campaign would be easy; a briefcase left on a train, conveniently discovered by a member of the public and containing juicy details of the celebrities and their tax avoidance schemes and he would make sure Bob

Hastings, Director General of the BBC was on that list of those under investigation. People would read the inevitable media reports and believe the whole story because they already knew part of it to be true. Benjamin would use old news to hide the lie. The Director General would deny the allegations, and his credibility would be undermined. The Government would then line up a few well-chosen backbenchers to demand his resignation in the public interest and with a new Director General in post, they would be in a position to influence the news output of one of the most trusted news services in the world, simple.

The second part of the plan would be some more difficult and require a bit of research. It would mean going back to the referendum results to find that suitably squalid little corner of England that voted to leave the EU; this bit of the story will be true. He would profile a few of the people that lived there and exaggerate how much better their lives would be after Brexit with projections of wealth, employment and reduced migration. This part of the story would be fake, but the new Director General will make sure the BBC runs the story over and over again. The Promised Land built on lies and deceit. The more Benjamin knew of the workings of the British government the more he agreed with the businessman and journalist Walter Bagehot who as far back as 1877, said that the inner circle of the Government, the Prime Minister's cabinet, was the *"efficient secret"*, keeping from the people what it didn't want them to know.

It took several days for the story about the Director General to break and the pro-government media went after Bob Hastings with a vengeance. They dug into his background, discovering a drink driving conviction from when he was a teenager in Leeds. This was a great bonus for Benjamin for it added more credibility to the story.

BBC News presenter Charlie Waits carried the story in the morning paper review along with guests John Wallaby and Robbie Lennon.

"And of course the main story in many of the papers this morning is that the Director General of the BBC, Mr. Bob Hastings, stands accused of tax avoidance. It seems confidential government papers were inadvertently left on the Waterloo Line yesterday morning and were picked up by a member of the public. They identify Bob Hastings, along with a couple of well-known celebrities, as being part of an elaborate scheme designed to defraud HMRC out of millions of pounds in unpaid tax. What's your take on this one, John?"

"Well, Charlie, I think the evidence here is irrefutable and that Bob Hastings needs to consider his position and resign as Director General immediately."

"And Robbie, should Bob Hastings resign?" "Absolutely, he's denied it of course but the evidence is clear; he's part of a scheme set up through a bank in the Cayman Islands that we know for a fact has been used for this purpose before. His position is untenable."

Charlie Waits nodded, "Yes, and I believe that the Right Honourable James Hatcher, MP for Rotherham, will today demand that the Prime Minister remove Bob Hastings and replace him with Sir Terrance McEvoy, a long-standing supporter of the Government."

The TV clicked off and Benjamin Rush pressed the intercom on his desk.

"Ms. Mortimer, get me Mary Joiner at Sky News then get a hold of Sir Terrance McEvoy. Drag him away from the golf course if you have to. Oh, and send a request over to CGRU for the results of the EU Referendum; I want the results for each of the 382 voting areas in the UK and I want these results cross-matrixed with socially deprived regions. Basically, I'm looking for poor people who voted 'leave' in the referendum. I need the results as soon as possible and if they give you any trouble tell them to contact Carol James for their P45."

The media hounded Bob Hastings and his family and inevitably Bob Hastings resigned a broken man with his reputation in ruins.

"Oh, hello Minister...is...ah...is there something I can do for you?" Benjamin Rush looked up as Carol James entered his office.

"No Benjamin not today. I just wanted to say well done on getting that extra Sky News piece on Bob Hastings. Certainly did the trick." She turned to leave, stopped, and turned around. "By the way, I got a call from John Barton down at CGRU; said you should be receiving an email from them any minute now and he apologised for the delay. Apparently, they were under the impression that I'd sack them if they didn't cooperate. Like I said, good work." Carol James smiled.

"Sir, we've got a Benjamin Rush requesting the EU referendum results." John Carter left his desk and walked over to Analyst Anthony David. "What do we know about Benjamin Rush?"

Anthony David tapped on his keyboard. "He's undersecretary to Carol James, Secretary of State for leaving the EU."

"Can we get a hold of these results too Anthony?"

"Yes Sir, we can intercept the email from the Central Government Research Unit and reroute it to your inbox so you'll get to see its contents before he does."

"Excellent, let's do that...and Anthony, this is on a need-to-know basis."

"Yes Sir."

When John Carter got the intercepted email from the CGRU to Benjamin Rush he placed a zip file attachment to it. The file looked like a little school satchel with the word 'Grabag' written on it. "Let's give you something to think about Benjamin Rush." John Carter mumbled to himself.

A ping from his inbox told Benjamin Rush that his request had been processed and the EU referendum results were in.

*Dear Mr. Rush*
*Please find attached a spreadsheet with the information you requested. I'd like to personally apologise for the delay in getting this information to you. If we can be of any further help please do not hesitate to get in touch.*
*Kind Regards*
*John Barton*
*CGRU Team Leader*

The Junior Minister may have long suspected that Government communications were subject to monitoring, but he didn't know that the use of any number of keywords would trigger an investigation by the ATU and a request for referendum results would certainly draw the attention of a section leader like John Carter.

He opened the spreadsheet and first on the list was Clacton-On-Sea. 50,000 people of voting age, high unemployment and migration 12% above the national average. Any attempt at helping the good people of Clacton-On-Sea had long been abandoned by successive governments and if Benjamin Rush could sell the Brexit dream here he could sell it anywhere.

The email contained a summary of the referendum results just as Benjamin had asked. It also contained the Grabag Zip File attachment. Benjamin's finger hovered over the Grabag icon for a few seconds before he clicked on it.

Full governmental information on all 382 voting areas, including Clacton-On-Sea, gathered into a PESTLE analysis of each area flashed up on the screen. This was standard research and analysis, based around the six pillars of confidence; Political, Economic, Social, Technological, Legal, and Environmental that

Government would use to track the impact of their policies or plans across the UK. There were archives of every story ever published about each area, every factory ever closed, and everyone who lost their homes when they lost their jobs and Benjamin Rush realised that it would be in these files that he would find the human-interest stories that he could manipulate into fake news for Carol James.

There was also a file entitled 'EU Referendum/Raw Data'. He clicked on that and another spreadsheet opened containing all 382 voting areas in the UK and against each name there was a breakdown of the voting pattern. Two columns were highlighted; percentage turnout and ballot box count. Benjamin Rush stared at the screen in disbelief as he scrolled down the results. He looked around his office and through the glass panels to the offices beyond.

He understood how the British voting system worked. It was a somewhat archaic system relying on paper trails and personal integrity rather than electronics and high-end security which to be fair could just as easily be hacked and manipulated as was seen in recent Presidential elections. In UK elections each voter arrives at the polling station, their identity is manually checked and verified and they are given a voting paper; in this case, a simple yes or no box to be ticked. They put their voting paper into a 'ballot box' and as each box gets filled it is sealed and a new one replaces it. At the end of the day the contents of each box is counted and for the referendum, the 'ballots' were put into three categories; 'yes', 'no', and 'spoiled'. These individual ballot box results are given to the local counting officer who adds all the box results together to produce the area result. This system has been in place largely unchanged since Henry Chapman invented the Ballot Box in 1856 for the general election of that year.

The percentage turnout of the voting population in each area is a relatively new addition to the voting system and is calculated independently of the ballot box count. It is inputted directly into a national database to give the percentage turnout figure so beloved by news outlets across the country. This is calculated by taking the number of people who voted on the day as a percentage of the number of people eligible to vote in that area. This percentage is sent to the Regional Counting Officer who announces the regional result for each of the twelve government regions across the UK and Northern Ireland and the national percentage turnout is then confirmed by the

Chairperson of the Electoral Commission. The vote and the turnout are two separate aspects of any election or referendum result and are operated independently of each other.

Benjamin Rush could see that in Clacton-on-Sea the total number of votes cast differed from the percentage turnout. Clacton-On-Sea while slightly lower than the national average had recorded a 70% turn out which meant that 35,000 people had checked in at the polling station and cast their vote but the ballot box totals showed 17,795 voting to leave the EU, 17,544 voting to remain, and 36 spoiled votes; a total of 35,375 votes had been counted; an extra 375 votes had been added to give a narrow victory to the leave campaign. Was this a cock-up or a conspiracy?

The only way to find out was to check all 382 voting areas so Benjamin Rush settled in for a long night at the office and in the morning he knew two things: 52 of the area results had been changed and the only people who could change the numbers in this way was the Local Counting Officers.

The second thing he knew was that someone had embedded that file in his report. He did not doubt that now his name was linked to this report and that he was in danger. The only way to save himself was to go public with the fact that Brexit was the biggest fake news story ever unleashed on the Great British public. Panicked, but trying to remain calm, he flicked through his contacts and called Jill Anderson at the London Standard.

"Hi Jill, it's Ben Rush here. You got a minute?"

"Hi Ben sure, always got time for an old friend."

"Listen, Jill could we meet tonight? Something's come across my desk that I think you might be interested in."

"Ah Ben, I'm up my neck in it here and I've a bit of me-time planned for tonight, maybe tomorrow?"

"This can't wait. I've evidence of voter fraud in the EU referendum. It shows that the results have been tampered with."

"Jesus Ben! And you're phoning me with this information! Is your line secure? Someone could be listening to this!"

"Yes, yes, don't worry. I'm routing the call through the Electron Encryption System."

"It better be secure Ben. I don't want a couple of grey suits knocking on my door some late night."

"You don't need to worry. Anyone listening to this will just hear a series of random words. You're perfectly safe. Trust me."

"I guess I am trusting you, I'll meet you tonight at 6 O'clock at the Goose and Hen pub on North End Road."

John Carter was listening, unfortunately for the Junior Minister he wasn't the only one. Benjamin Rush downloaded the documents onto a flash drive and left for his appointment with Jill Anderson. Little did he know that the Electron Encryption System wasn't all it was cracked up to be.

## Chapter Four

Jim Brannigan sat at the kitchen table in John Carter's apartment and scribbled Michael Logan's name on a piece of paper and drew lines off to John Carter, Annette Chambers, Sir Alistair McIntyre, SUV driver, Pawn Ticket, and Benjamin Rush. He redrew the line between Michael Logan, Sir Alistair, and Benjamin Rush. He circled Sir Alistair's name over and over again.

He checked his watch and burned the paper with his lighter. Dealing with Chambers would have to wait: he had to focus on what he knew or at least suspected, that she worked for Sir Alistair McIntyre and that pointed to ATU involvement.

Carter's apartment had been cleaned and not in a 'didn't the maid do a good job' kind of a way more like a 'let's remove any DNA' kind of way: so John Carter was either being held against his will or he was dead. Again, that pointed to one of the secret service departments being involved.

Chambers was surprised when Brannigan turned up at the apartment which meant she wasn't expecting him, at least not yet, which meant he wasn't being followed by ATU. She was there either looking for something like a laptop or planting something like a pawn ticket.

Maybe she knew Brannigan would call at some point: but since the pawn ticket would have taken a day or so to set up none of this was last minute which meant there was a plan in play.

He felt he was in a web of some sort and his gut told him that McIntyre was the spider, weaving his evil web through people's lives, destroying them as he went. Then there was the fact that Chambers recognised Brannigan, maybe from some report or briefing, and again that pointed to the secret service, also probably ATU. He had never come across her before but it's a huge organisation, stretching across the Globe so that wouldn't mean anything in itself.

And finally there was Benjamin Rush.... all Brannigan knew was that he had been drugged and left in the hotel room to be killed. That in itself wasn't unusual, ATU was built on secrecy. It was, by its very nature, compartmentalised so no one person ever had an overview of how the jigsaw pieces fitted together; except Sir Alistair of course. All he knew for definite was that ATU was involved with Carter and Rush. And since terror and the illusion of terrorism was their thing, probably with Michael as well, and now so was he, which meant he could be in a bit of trouble. Everything he knew or suspected was tied to a little man in a grey building in Vauxhall.

He'd be a sitting target if someone came calling in the middle of the night, so he left quietly and made his way across the city to the voice on the other end of the phone.

Susan Blakeshaw lived in a quiet cul-de-sac in the Waterloo borough of London. Seven little detached bungalows built long ago and now surrounded by glass and steel.

She had bought this house straight out of University, so while friends of hers were backpacking around the world to find themselves she was nest building in her favourite place in the World. She had grown up here with her mother, her father, and her sister; four people so wrapped up in each other it was as though the rest of the world simply didn't exist. It's fair to say they lived a blissful life, the sort that only wealth can provide.

Her potential was spotted at University, top of her class in computer programming, problem-solving, and analysis. She was approached by one of her professors to consider joining a new government agency that was being set up to promote British interests around the world and help combat the ever-growing terrorist threat, both domestic and foreign.

Her parents were somewhat disappointed when she became a civil servant and they were concerned she'd wasted her potential. Still, they loved her and that's all that mattered. That is until her mother died and her father remarried. He devoted himself to his new wife, a ghastly woman named Beatrice and the sisters sought solace in each other and remained best friends until the cold wind of change once again blew through their lives.

In those days Susan had wanted a family of her own, a husband, possibly a couple of kids, and of course a home in Waterloo. She got the home.

Number four Waterloo Gardens had bright white paintwork, window boxes and a neat lawn that gave the property that cared-for look. Brannigan parked on the street directly outside and walked up the short path to the front door.

The door opened just as he put his finger on the doorbell. "What kept you?" she said angrily, "I've been looking out for you, expected you earlier".

Apart from the necessary phone calls as Brannigan's analyst they had neither spoken nor seen each other for the last two years.

Susan looked older than he remembered. Wisps of grey laced through jet-black hair like cream through coffee and wrinkles danced around her eyes. But she was still beautiful, with clear skin void of the concealment of makeup, crystal-blue eyes and high cheekbones. She was slim and tall and even from the front door she smelled wonderful and she reminded him of Jennifer. Susan was Jennifer's younger sister by a few years. Their mother Jean died ten years ago, and their Father was, the last time anyone heard, living on a yacht with Beatrice somewhere in the Canary Islands.

Susan let the front door swing open and walked to the far corner of the living room. She stared out into the garden and kept her back to Brannigan, he stepped into the middle of the room and waited on the offer of a seat, but the offer didn't come.

"What was Michael mixed up in?" she said eventually. There was sadness in her voice and Brannigan detected a trace of guilt there too.

`"I don't know, but he was no terrorist, and John's missing." Brannigan let the statement hang in the air but Susan didn't respond and the silence between them grew in the fading light of day, broken only by the faint ticking of the grandfather clock that stood to attention in the far-left corner of the room.

"Michael had been working for John" Susan said softly, as though saying it aloud would shatter any last hope that Michael's death and John's disappearance weren't linked.

"When were they last in touch with you?" Brannigan was curious now to find out what Susan knew.

"John used to call round now and then. He said Michael wasn't coping well after the accident. He thought I should maybe reach out to him."

"And did you?"

"I just couldn't, you know that. I still blamed him for Jennifer's death. My only sister and he took her from me. I trusted him for Christ's sake. Hell, I even loved him..I thought he loved me too."

Brannigan sat down on the sofa. Susan turned with tears in her eyes and joined him.

Jennifer had been killed in a car accident two years ago when the car she was a passenger in collided with an articulated lorry at the junction of Forest Road and Chingford Road, Walthamstow late one Wednesday night. Michael had been driving and he had been drinking. They had been out together a couple of times and he had hopes it could lead to something more permanent. But it wasn't to be.

As they sat on the sofa Brannigan told Susan all he knew, well almost. He told her about seeing Michael's photo on the news, about meeting Annette Chambers at John's apartment and about the ticket to Edinburgh. He didn't tell her that he had just killed a Government Minister, but he did tell her that his apartment had been trashed.

"Look Susan, the way I see it is that Sir Alistair McIntyre is the key to all of this. He's the one person that links everything and everybody. You work for ATU, same as me and you know how these things are done, everyone working on seemingly random pieces of work but only one person seeing the whole jigsaw. And that person is Sir Alistair McIntyre."

"But why?" she asked.

"You're the analyst; I was hoping you'd tell me."

Susan sat silently for a few moments.

"Well, I see the Prime Minster is outlining plans for tighter border controls and a curb on immigration. They'll probably use Michael as the poster boy for what frightens us the most; the modern-day bogyman, the home-grown terrorist. This could help them bring in emergency laws for every citizen to carry photo ID cards. There's even talk about restricting movement across the country. The two scenarios we were working on to create this 'Neo-Democratic State' was terrorism or some sort of virus pandemic." Susan sat quietly, again thinking about all that had just been said.

Her job was to connect seemingly random events, sometimes even making them seem random to progress the Government's agenda. She was also Brannigan's point of contact. Every field agent had one person that they linked to within ATU, and in the beginning it seemed natural that Susan would be Jim's designated analyst.

"John was quite vocal in his concerns about how the public was being manipulated by the Government and that got him noticed. I think he wanted out. I think he knew he was putting himself in danger. Maybe that's why he's in hiding. And now you're being pushed toward Edinburgh, that makes no sense," she said. "There's an international Climate Change Summit in Edinburgh Castle this weekend with delegates from across Europe, the Middle East, and China attending. Since the Paris agreement there's real concern about Global Warming but what has that got to do with ATU, or John, or you for that matter? Besides, I hope you not planning on staying there tomorrow, there won't be a room within fifty miles of the city." She smiled weakly.

Brannigan wanted to ask what a Neo-Democratic State was but was too tired, too tired to worry about tomorrow. "Susan, can I stay the night?" It came out more as a plea than a question. "I have to be at the bus station first thing, you won't even have to make me breakfast." That weak smile flickered across her face again but died quickly on the corners of her mouth.

"Spare room's made up, one next to mine; first door on the left passed the bathroom."

Brannigan began to stand when Susan gently put her hand on his.

"Jim, I don't blame you for what happened between Michael and Jennifer. I know I haven't seen you since the funeral and I'm not even sure why I agreed to continue to be your analyst. I think hearing your voice over the phone somehow kept me connected to Jennifer."

She hadn't called him Jim since the funeral and there was warmth in the way she said it and he was grateful for that but he felt their friendship died with Jennifer.

**Day Three: The Offence**

At 2 am precisely the lock on the front door turned slowly and silently and the door was eased open to allow the two masked figures to move quietly into the apartment. Both wore identical assault kits; full body, black combat tactical uniform, bullet-proof vest, and gloves. One was slightly taller than the other and each had matching Smith & Wesson MK-22s with suppressor attached. The shorter of the two was first in and took up position immediately inside the front door, scanning the room and the kitchen beyond for any sign of movement. When the second assassin entered they made their way slowly down the corridor and passed the bathroom, each one taking up position outside a bedroom door. The taller figure raised a fist and then held up three fingers indicating three seconds to contact. Two, one, and the bedroom doors were kicked open. Bullets exploded into the beds and the contents of the duvets spewed into the air like confetti. But the shooting stopped almost as soon as it started. The beds were empty and the assassins moved back into the living room.

The taller one pulled off the balaclava.

"Shit! Where the fuck is he?!" screamed Annette Chambers. They both left John Carter's apartment for the waiting SUV.

"Is it done?" Sir Alistair McIntyre was sitting in the front passenger seat as Annette Chambers and Special Agent Matt Jones climbed into the back of the SUV.

"No, he wasn't there," she replied as the car pulled slowly away and took a left into Warwick Street.

"Well then, we'll need to progress as planned. Get Carter's body into place and we'll let the Anti-terrorist police pick Brannigan up in Edinburgh. Let me out here."

The vehicle stopped outside The Garrick, a private members club in Soho with an unremarkable frontage except for the crest above the door; a golden silhouette of a single turret Roman Fort. McIntyre didn't say goodbye and made no gesture of recognition to the doorman as he entered the building.

Brannigan was gone when Susan checked on him the next morning and, in truth, she was relieved not to have to talk to him. She had found the previous night difficult with too many painful memories dragged up. She thought of Michael and the betrayal she felt when she discovered he had been cheating on her with Jennifer and the hatred she had for her sister. But that knowledge only came with the accident and the subsequent police investigation and her sister was far beyond her anger. She blamed Brannigan too in a way. If he had been a better husband then perhaps Jennifer wouldn't have looked elsewhere for love or companionship but that morning she blamed herself for the spitefulness of her thoughts. She poured herself a coffee and switched on the television. Pictures of Edinburgh Castle filled the screen.

"*It was at exactly 7.14 am this morning when a suspected masked terrorist killed three members of the Chinese delegation attending the Climate Change Summit here in Edinburgh Castle today,*" said the reporter. "*After running down a service corridor to avoid capture the hooded suspect then blew himself up before he could be arrested. He has been named as John Carter, a kitchen porter at the castle who may have links to another home-grown terrorist, Michael Logan, who recently blew up the Vanderbilt building in London killing all 35 residents. Police believe these men are part of a new terrorist network operating in the Capital and have taken the unusual step of issuing a photo of a third suspect they are looking for in connection with these attacks. He is to be considered armed and dangerous and must not be approached by the public.*"

An old army photo of Jim Brannigan flashed up on the screen.

"Oh my God!" said Susan and she dialled Brannigan's number.

## Chapter Five

The 6.45 am Edinburgh Express from London left on time with Jim Brannigan on board weighing up his somewhat limited options. He had no idea what he was going to do when he got to Edinburgh; he had no way of contacting John Carter even if he was in Edinburgh and still alive. If Susan was right and the Government was using the intelligent services to orchestrate terrorist attacks to destabilise the United Kingdom and pursue its own agenda of creating this new Neo-Democratic Independent UK with federal laws to control its citizens, then anything was possible.

The truth was he never listened to the news, never read the papers and never kept up to date with world affairs. He just didn't give a damn and he understood in that way he was no different to millions of others. This dumbing down created a vacuum that allowed fake news to be born. The great British public was being spoon-fed this shit every day. It was no wonder politicians could do what they wanted; no wonder they manipulated everything: we let them get away with it after all.

He had to find John Carter one way or the other and get to the bottom of whatever he and Michael had been working on, and then he had to find out why the Right Honourable Benjamin Rush had to die. At least he was in the clear.

He hadn't slept well in Susan's house. He was half expecting a couple of heavily armed midnight callers to kick down the front door and drag them both off in handcuffs or kill them where they slept. It would be another six or seven hours before the bus reached Edinburgh and that meant now at last he could get some sleep.

He was wakened shortly after 8.30 am by the gentle buzzing of his mobile… "Jim." This time there was no warmth in her voice when she said his name only a sense of urgency and fear.

"It's all over the news, John's dead. They're saying he was the suicide bomber that killed three Chinese delegates in Edinburgh this morning and then blew himself up. They're looking for a third man in connection with this attack and the one in London. It's you, Jim, they're looking for you! They've released your picture and they say you're armed and dangerous and must not be approached. Anyone who sees you is to contact the police immediately."

"Susan, you need to go." This was no time to be emotional, because that would let in anger and fear and he knew that these old enemies would cloud his judgment. "Time we started playing offence. I need to see a man about a murder but first I have to get off this damn bus."

"But Jim, you're a terrorist now. Every camera in the country will be looking for you, any face in the crowd might recognise you."

"Susan, you need to go." He hung up without waiting for a response. She knew what she had to do.

Brannigan knew they'd find him, this was now a man-hunt and he had to get ahead of the game. He'd been pushed and now he was being chased but who were they? ATU of course, but he wondered if any other Government branch might be involved.

At the end of the Second World War there had been seventeen Military Intelligence sections at the War Office but now there were only four: MI5, who were the National Security Agency dealing with covert threats against the UK: MI6, the Secret Intelligence Agency dealing with regional instability across the world; GCHQ who collect intelligence relevant to UK policy around the world and ATU, perhaps the most secretive of all the agencies. Their brief is to protect UK interests and policy by controlling the threat of terrorism at home and abroad.

Jim had been part of this agency for years, as had John and Susan. They were data capture and analysis while he was a field agent but they all knew what they were doing: manipulation of domestic and world events to further UK interests.

ATU was behind this he was sure. Michael was killed because he helped John, John had been killed because he did something he shouldn't have and that was the key to this mess. He had been dragged into it because ATU knew he would investigate their deaths and the only person who could make such a decision was Sir Alistair McIntyre, ATU Headquarters, Vauxhall Cross, London and it was to there that Jim needed to go. The only problem was the small inconvenience that he was now on an Express Bus to Edinburgh, that he was going there because of a pawn ticket he had been given by Annette Chambers, who probably worked for McIntyre, and they now wanted him dead, so he had to get off that bloody bus!

Luckily there weren't too many people on board and most of them were asleep, so he reckoned he'd be okay for a while.

"Hey Mister, you're on the news." The voice came from the seat behind and the accent was unmistakeably Glaswegian; thick and deep with that distinctive trilling on the 'r' of Mister. "Hey Pal, I'm talking to you."

The voice was now to Jim's left, its owner blocking out the early morning sun while he held the screen of his phone toward Jim. "That's you, innit?" It took an almost unnecessary glance out of the corner of his eye to confirm it was indeed his photo, taken from his army file and a little dated now but definitely Jim Brannigan, UK's most wanted terrorist.

One swift and forceful fist to the groin rendered the man speechless and bent him in two. A hard shoulder shove into the empty seat opposite took him out of sight completely and a tight clamp over his mouth completed the task. Now it only required a nose pinch and the big man from Glasgow was flapping like a fish on the end of a hook, his eyes bulging with the realisation that he was dying.

But Jim Brannigan didn't want him dead. This was his way off the damned bus. He tapped the passenger in the seat in front of him on the shoulder. "This man's not well, I think he may be having an attack of some sort."

The passenger jumped up, took one look at the big man from Glasgow and shouted, "Help, help. This man's having a heart attack".

The bus screeched to a halt, and the driver pushed his way up the bus, defibrillator in hand.

"Let me through, let me through!" he shouted. Some of the passengers had stood up and moved into the aisle to get a better look but now backed into their seats to allow the driver through.

In the confusion and panic, Jim Brannigan moved down the bus, pushed the lever to open the door and stepped out onto the hard shoulder of the A1 motorway. The Motorway sign indicated that Durham was the next exit. He hopped over the security barrier, pulled his coat tight against the cold of a winter's morning, and made his way across the open countryside toward Durham and onward to London for an unscheduled meeting in Vauxhall Cross.

Being wanted by the police in the United Kingdom means you have to do the impossible; disappear while everyone is watching. Not just the 4.9 million CCTV cameras operating on every street corner but the digital traces we all leave in our daily lives almost minute by minute, day by day. Jim Brannigan knew this only too well, that's one reason he didn't own a laptop, or a smartphone, or have anything as ridiculous a social network profile. But even he had to use a bank card, a driver's licence, or a passport occasionally. In his case, these were usually fake, but they too could still be tracked.

Many of the people on the National Crime Agency's most wanted list had disappeared decades ago, never to be found. The problem he had was that they put the word terrorist in front of his name which meant that everyone would be looking for him. Every face in every crowd at every bus station, train station, or airport in the country could recognise him.

Over time he had developed a sixth sense about being followed, a gut feeling that had served him well over the years. He could recognise law enforcement instinctively; he recognised them on their days off shopping with their wife and kids; he recognised them by the way they walked and the way they talked. He should do for Christ's sake, after all, he had been one of them for a very long time.

He figured that this lifetime experience would serve him well in the days to come and maybe give him an edge when he needed it most. That and a well-serviced Glock 17 pistol. Nevertheless he had to stay hidden, using public transport only when absolutely necessary and even then seeking out isolated bus or train stops to reduce the chances of being spotted.

It's a long way from Edinburgh to London, some 400 miles as the crow flies and even though he was some way off the Scottish Border he was no crow. He would have to keep to minor roads if he was to make it safely to Durham. Durham was famous for two things; a Cathedral and a University and that would mean lots of people. Students and tourists mingling with locals filling the streets, cafes and hotels. This would be somewhere he could hide in plain sight.

It took two hours and eight miles of walking before he heard the unmistakable rattle of an old Ford Transit minibus thundering towards him. Brannigan decided to take a risk and stuck his thumb out. The minibus from Durham University Sub-Aqua Club braked hard and came to a halt a few yards up the road. The side door slid open and a rather attractive girl popped her head out of the minibus. "Hiya, I'm Laura. Jump in." Brannigan sat in the single seat beside the sliding door. "Where are you going to?" shouted the driver. "Anywhere near the train station would be great" "No problem" came the friendly reply.

The minibus was full of students talking and laughing loudly. Laura sat opposite Brannigan. "We're on our way back from Scapa Flow, exploring the wrecks of the German battle fleet from the war. Diving's great up there this time of year. Do you Scuba Dive?"
"Never seemed to find the time," shouted Brannigan above the noise.

They were a friendly bunch and not too inquisitive about where he was going or where he'd come from. Instead, they were more interested in telling him about their weekend and he was more than happy to listen. They did ask him to 'like them' the next time he was on his online profile but by and large they talked about themselves and made fun of Mark, a tall skinny kid in the front of the minibus who got drunk and made a fool of himself with Laura, who seemed a few years older and wiser than the tall skinny kid in the front of the minibus.

"Hey Laura, watch out Mark doesn't catch you talking to this dude!" shouted one of the two students sitting directly behind her. That started roars of laughter and howling from the other students. Laura looked embarrassed.

"Why don't you shut the fuck up, Peter!" She then looked over to Brannigan "Mark tried it on with me last night."

"Yea and Laura here choked him right out. Didn't you darling?" laughed Peter. "Mark's eyes rolled back in his head like he was having an orgasm, then he passed out! Poor bastard didn't even enjoy himself." More roaring and laughter. "Or maybe Laura was playing one of her erotica-asphyxiation games? Like the one we heard about on the radio this morning with that politician?"

"Why don't you two bobble heads piss off!" shouted Laura, anger now adding to her embarrassment that only served to generate a whole new bunch of Oohs and Ahs from the students.

"Politician?" asked Brannigan.

"Some guy found dead in Soho over the weekend," said Laura "Police said it was a case of some kinky sex game gone wrong. The sleazy bastard had a reputation for preying on young women. Said on the news he was a Junior Minister in the Government. Wouldn't surprise me, they're all the same."
"Men or Junior Ministers?" asked Brannigan with a smile. Laura laughed, "Both! Gaud, I hope you're not one, are you?"
"Well, yes and no." They both laughed. "Okay fella, this is your stop."

The minibus pulled up outside Durham train station and Brannigan jumped out to join the hordes of visitors exploring the pretty cobbled streets. At the nearest bus stop a glance at the timetable told him that the next bus due was going to Oxford, another University City. He got on and from there he caught a half-empty late evening train to Waterloo and then walked the last few miles toward ATU headquarters.

It was getting dark when he eventually arrived in Vauxhall; he couldn't go back to Susan's in case it was being watched so on impulse he walked toward the Apollo Guest House on Durham Street. Some of the letters above the door were broken and the word 'OLL' shone out across the street. A 'Rooms Available' sign fought for its life in the window. He sighed and pushed hard on the front door.

A Shane McGowan lookalike with bad teeth and an attitude to match sat behind a small reception desk. A sheet of plate glass separated him from whatever the night air might blow in.

"Room please," said Brannigan

"By the hour or the night?"

Brannigan laughed to himself "Well, Booking.Com never mentioned you rent by the hour so I guess I'll take a whole night."

The young man turned to get a key, "Arse hole."

"What's that?" asked Brannigan.

"I said no breakfast, no towels, and no hookers."

"What? You don't supply hookers? That's going to affect your Trip Advisor score."

"Look Mister, you trying to be funny? It's thirty-five quid for the night and before you ask we don't take Visa."

Vauxhall is a mixed commercial and residential district of London in the Borough of Lambeth and for most people it's just a stop on the Victoria Line on their way to somewhere else. It has a reputation for being more than a little rough around the edges and most people who live there don't do so out of choice, so it's a perfect place to hide a large grey building with a large grey front door that houses some of the most secretive Government agencies in the UK and field offices for around 30 other countries, all working together to control world economies through the apparent chaos of modern warfare and fear.

The whole of the third floor was occupied by the Anti-Terrorist Unit. Not that you'd know any of this from the outside because there were no signs saying 'ATU This Way', no bells to push, and no brass name-plates to polish, just a card swipe like you have on hotel bedroom doors.

This building didn't even have a name or postcode because it didn't exist. In fact, if you needed to ask anything about this building then you really shouldn't be anywhere near it, but then Jim Brannigan didn't need to ask any questions.

He knew it would be impossible to get in undetected using his ID as it was surely red-flagged. He also knew that Sir Alistair McIntyre didn't use the big grey door preferring instead to use an underground service passage that lead from Vauxhall Tube Station to directly under the building with a service elevator at the far end going only to the third floor.

Brannigan lay on the single bed in the squalid room at the Apollo and let the curtains hang open. The lights and sounds of the city seeped into the room giving it a yellow, jaundiced hew. He sighed and got up to look out of the window. A night in the Apollo dragged on like a fortnight in jail, dull and boring with the occasional screams and shouts from the darkness outside.

By 4 am exhaustion had given way to frustration. Brannigan closed the creaking door as quietly as he could and headed out for a late-night stroll into the neon-infested streets.

Late-nighters in any city fall into two distinct groups: those who want to be out late and those who have to be out late either because they are working or they're homeless. The pubs and clubs vibrated to loud music and the sounds of people enjoying themselves, although with the screaming and shouting going on Brannigan wasn't sure if they were enjoying themselves or fighting for their lives. He guessed it was probably the former as there was no sign of armed police at any of the

venues just yet. When he looked down the alleyways and into the doorways he could see the faces of despair and pain that go with life on the streets. Here and there a few well-meaning people in uniform praised the Lord and give out blankets and soup and the night dragged on. His phone pinged:
*Tube from Waterloo, 6.15 am tomorrow morning. Intercept at Vauxhall. Susan*

So a plan was in motion, if he was to intercept Sir Alistair and get the information he needed then he'd have to be at Vauxhall tube station for the 6.15 am tube from Waterloo tomorrow morning. And he'd have to get caught.

## Day Four: The Defence

Brannigan got back in time for a shower and a shave before heading down into Marlborough tube station and off to Vauxhall Cross. At 6.15am Sir Alistair McIntyre stepped off the train and into the early morning throng battling their way to God knows where. But he hardly seemed to notice as he strode purposefully through the crowd and toward Brannigan who was leaning idly against a pillar reading a newspaper.

"My dear boy" he started. "It's so good to see you, we missed you in Edinburgh."

It was then that Brannigan felt the unmistakeable pressure of a Smith and Wesson pistol in the small of his back and Special Agent Matt Jones slipped his hand into Brannigan's jacket and relieved him of his Glock. He knew it was coming. He'd spotted Agents Millar and Roberts sitting at the Coffee Dock and they had spotted him no doubt. They probably contacted McIntyre on the train and their trap was set. The agent coming in from behind was a nice touch though he thought. "That little diversion on the bus was very clever. Still, we have you now." McIntyre walked off and the prod in the back meant it was time for Brannigan to follow. Millar and Roberts fell in behind.

In that moment time slowed as it often does when one needs to process information in the split of a second, consider options and make a decision. He wanted to get caught: he needed to get caught but he was now wondering if going into one of the most secure buildings in the world was really a smart move. The gun in the back would be no problem, neither would any resistance he might get from McIntyre or the two agents but he didn't want any more casualties from this mess and with this many people around he couldn't be certain of that. He could always kill them later in the tunnel if he changed his mind and besides this way he might get some answers.

## Chapter Six

The old lift groaned its way up to the third floor and, in a seemingly final act of exhaustion, slipped ever so slightly backward as its doors wheezed open and McIntyre stepped out.

The whole floor was a hum of activity; the huge open-plan space was awash with TVs and computer screens, each one attached to the desk of an analyst like Susan. Their job was to monitor news feeds, financial markets, war zones, political elections and just about everything that took place in the world. They looked for patterns or opportunities and would feed back every day to their section supervisors, who in turn reported to the Head of Cyber Terrorism and upwards to Sir Alistair McIntyre. It was on these reports that decisions were made and fake news was born.

Four small rooms like glass cubes stood in each corner of the floor. Each one contained a small black leather sofa, a table, two chairs, a computer and a secure phone line. They were soundproofed and at the touch of the little button on the underside of the desk, the glass could be tinted against prying eyes. Each door was numbered one to four in a clockwise manner.

The troop made their way across the floor to room one. Agents Millar and Roberts took up positions outside like modern-day centurions guarding Cesar's tent. McIntyre sat in the chair on the far side of the table so that he was facing the door and he motioned for Brannigan to take the other chair. Special Agent Matt Jones took the sofa. Brannigan stood.

"Well, you're supposed to be dead" began McIntyre, "Shot by our wonderful anti-terrorist police while attempting to blow up Edinburgh Bus Station yesterday in a revenge attack for the deaths of your friends. We had the news release ready, but you didn't show."

He sounded like he was disappointed at the wasted effort. If he was expecting a conversation then he was going to be disappointed. He did pause for a second but when Brannigan didn't speak he continued on a different tack. "I'm sorry about all this, I always liked you, honest." His mouth said one thing but his eyes said another, they were cold, and empty and Brannigan knew then that he may not live very much longer.

"Why?" he asked.

"Why what?" replied McIntyre. "Why are you here? Or why did we frame Carter for the murder of some Chinese delegates in Edinburgh? Or why that drunk Logan is suddenly part of a terrorist network? Or why you are going to die?"

"Why?" repeated Brannigan.

"I'll tell you why. Because it's my job to keep this country safe and its people under control. Not the Government's or the politicians but mine and when John Carter grew a conscience and decided to send Benjamin Rush the complete raw data on the Referendum results, he set in motion a chain of events that couldn't be stopped.

You see, it was Carter's responsibility to monitor everything connected to Brexit including requests for information across all Government departments. Somewhere along the line, he made a decision that cost him his life and the lives of so many others. It wasn't just Benjamin Rush he sent the information to. Then he sent Logan to make sure Rush met that reporter woman, Anderson. And that's when you got dragged into this little drama. We were already planning to increase the terrorist threat in London so we drew up a plan, a quite ingenious plan, to link this all together and get rid of Carter in the process. We created a fake news story about a terrorist cell of old army buddies radicalised by Islam extremists."

Brannigan interrupted, "Who is this 'we' you keep referring to?"

"Well I guess it doesn't matter now. It was me and Carter's boss, the head of Cyber terrorism here at ATU. We knew once you realised your friends were dying you would start looking for answers and hopefully help us find that damned laptop, but you disappointed, dear boy. Instead, you went off to see Susan Blakeshaw and that's when I had the idea of using you as part of the terrorist cell so that we could get rid of you too at the same time. So, you see John Carter brought you here and John Carter got you killed."

"Wrong," said Brannigan. "I brought myself here and I'm not the one who got killed."

As Matt Jones leaped to his feet, Brannigan took one step forward and with a springing action off his heels head-butted the agent full on the nose.

A head butt is a much-undervalued attack method but if delivered correctly it can be amazingly effective and debilitating. The forehead is hard and the neck muscles can put your full force behind the strike. Most people are taken by surprise because they expect you to raise your arms or use your fists; they don't expect you to use your head. However, that's just what Brannigan did and Matt Jones' face caved in.

His nose was smashed, cheekbones fractured, blood flooded into his throat and he had difficulty breathing. He dropped to his knees and then onto the floor, unconscious. Brannigan was already beside a startled Sir Alistair and hit the button on the underside of the desk, tinting the glass. No one could see in but he could still see out and luckily no one was coming his way. He had taken a risk hitting Jones in plain sight like that but for once his luck held.

He grabbed McIntyre by his Windsor knot and pushed it into his Adam's apple, crushing it in the process and lifting Sir Alistair onto the tip-toes of his well-polished Oxford Brogues so that he couldn't speak or move. The only problem was that Brannigan was now trapped in a glass cube inside one of the most secretive and secure buildings in the UK with two agents at the door and his only exit was a creaking lift on the other side of a vast open plan office that led down to the London Underground.

He had to get out and he'd need McIntyre to do this safely and quietly, so he couldn't kill him just yet. The only way for him to survive beyond today was to get some insurance and disappear. He needed the information that got John Carter killed.

"We're leaving this room and heading for the lift. Anything about you causes me concern and I'll kill you, understand?" He knew he didn't need to say that last bit but it felt good to say it out loud.

Sir Alistair nodded and Brannigan loosened his grip on the Windsor knot causing him to rock back off his tiptoes and then slump forward, gasping for breath and holding onto the desk to prevent himself from collapsing beside Special Agent Jones. He glared at Brannigan but didn't speak, he knew better.

The odds were currently in favour of him staying alive, but he also knew that if he did anything to change those odds then he could just as easily die. So he stayed quiet.

Brannigan flipped the unconscious Matt Jones onto his side and took the agent's ID and gun. He also retrieved his Glock." Is Chambers in the building?"

"I believe so," croaked Sir Alistair, rubbing his throat.

"When we get to the elevator get the agents to contact her. Tell her to meet you at the Coffee Dock in fifteen minutes with the Carter file."

Now it was Sir Alistair's turn to say nothing. Brannigan shoved the Glock into his gut and threatened him through clenched teeth.

"Nod, God dam you or I'll kill you where you stand and take my chances outside." McIntyre nodded almost unperceivably. "Stay in front of me like before and do nothing that'll cost you your life."

He opened the door of the cube and McIntyre stepped out first, Brannigan followed and the two agents fell in behind once again. No one asked about Special Agent Jones. At the lift, McIntyre instructed the agents as he had been told and called the lift up to the third floor.

"But Sir," replied Agent Millar "personnel files are not to leave the building."

"Don't argue with me, agent! I wrote the damn rule book! And tell her to hurry up."
The two men stepped inside the lift and began their descent to the service tunnel in silence.

"What do you think you're doing?" asked McIntyre eventually, "You think taking me as some sort of hostage will help you? You have gotten out of the building but you're still a dead man walking".

"Maybe I am and that's okay, but you'll pay for what you've done!" Brannigan found himself shouting, almost out of control. He was shocked to hear his angry voice and surprised for he knew that the only way to survive was to be in control, always.

The lift door clunked open, and the two men walked along the service tunnel and onward to the Coffee Dock. Brannigan reckoned they'd have found Special Agent Jones by now, realised what happened and be flooding the area with agents. Still, he had the Director of

ATU at gunpoint and they were in a public place, so he'd have to see how this one would play out.

He'd get the file from Annette Chambers, get on the next tube with McIntyre and try and lose them somewhere along the line. He knew it was weak, but it was all he had.

"You stay close to me and I won't hurt you," said Brannigan.

"It's not you I'm worried about dear boy" replied Sir Alistair.

Brannigan and Sir Alistair were seated at the coffee dock for only a few moments when Annette Chambers walked slowly, almost casually, toward them through the morning crowd.

Brannigan turned to Sir Alistair. "It always amazed me that an agency built on secrecy and whose sole purpose is subversion should still keep paper files."
"A throwback to a different time I guess" he replied, "Maybe old habits really do die hard after all, like old agents."

Annette Chambers was tall and elegant with a tan leather bag slung over her left shoulder. She seemed relaxed and smiled at McIntyre. He smiled nervously back as her right hand came across her abdomen and slid into the bag. She drew the gun, a Sig Sauer P238 with silencer, and before Brannigan could raise his Glock she pumped three bullets into McIntyre's chest. He stared blankly forward, his eyes, thought Brannigan, no different in death than they had been in life really; blank and cold.

"If you want to live, follow me," she said.

A woman at the table opposite looked up from her morning Latte as she heard the popping sound of the silencer. She seemed not to register the scene unfolding in front of her as blood appeared in three little pools on McIntyre's crisp white shirt before seeming to reach out to each other to make one large red mass of death.

At the same time, Brannigan could see Millar and Roberts moving fast through the crowd behind Annette Chambers; guns drawn, their arms hanging casually by their sides and their long black overcoats providing a degree of camouflage for the weapons.

A man with a briefcase followed the woman's gaze to Sir Alistair's blood-soaked shirt and turned to run, knocking the woman behind him into one of the tables. People began running in all directions. Then the screaming started, and then the panic.

It's a well-documented fact that people have a herd mentality when they find themselves in a stressful situation. One spooked individual can stampede a whole crowd resulting in injury and death, like the stampede in October 2016 in Ethiopia where 300 people were killed during the annual festival of thanksgiving.

Turning panic into a stampede to avoid capture or hide evidence however is quite often used by law enforcement. So when the man with the briefcase followed the woman's gaze to McIntyre's blood-soaked shirt and then turned and started running he triggered a chain reaction through the crowd at Vauxhall tube station that Brannigan knew might just save his life.

People began running in all directions, most of them not even sure why they were running; the herd was on the move. Chambers grabbed Brannigan by the arm "Let's go!" she shouted, and they ran toward an exit and away from the suits with guns. Up the stairs, two at a time, pushing past those people not running fast enough or not running at all, pushing up into the daylight and a chance to get lost on busy London streets.

They burst out of the tube station along with hundreds of others and they kept running; down streets, zigzagging through traffic, heading nowhere in particular. When they thought they were far enough away they slowed down and walked quickly side by side, Chambers dropped her gun into a street bin before they dodged into a Debenhams' department store and found a table in the little café at the back; just two people having coffee a long way from a dead man in the London Underground.

"You mind telling me what just happened?" asked Brannigan.

"Once we discovered Matt Jones in the cube we knew McIntyre had been compromised," Chambers began, "I was sent to kill you both and I would have until I saw the two Agents tailing me and realised that this was to be a 3-way hit. I shoot you two and then I'm shot by 'anti-terrorist police' operating on the Underground and then they create some bullshit story about me being a terrorist."

"I know how you feel," mumbled Brannigan

"Another fake news story to cover up the truth," Chambers continued, "I took a risk that you might be the only chance I now have of staying alive. Hope I was right. Besides, you and I need to work together."

"Why would I do that?" said Brannigan.

"The way I see it, we both want the same thing."

"And what is that exactly?"

"To find Carter's Laptop, use it as leverage and save ourselves." said Chambers.

"So, they're cleaning up, but I thought we were they. Who gave you the order?" asked Brannigan

"It came through the secure line, from the office of the Secretary of State for Exiting the European Union."

"You think the Minister herself gave the order?"

"I don't know, but anything's possible"

There comes a time when running is no longer an option because the chasing won't stop until you stop it. You must decide to either give up and disappear or take the fight to the enemy and Jim Brannigan wasn't about to give up or disappear, not when they killed his friends and put him on the UK's most wanted list.

"What's in the file?" he asked.

"Everything" replied Chambers "The Brexit referendum results, Logan and Carter's death, smear campaigns against everyone who got in the way, everything"

"And Carol James, how do we find her?" asked Brannigan.

"She's in the file too."

Chambers took the file out of her tan leather bag and handed it to Brannigan. It was a small plastic zip file and it was slimmer than he imagined.

"You'd have thought that with so many dead there would be more paperwork," said Brannigan. He flicked through it, "She lives in Compton Avenue, London N6, number 13. Unlucky for some," he said with a wry smile. "Right then, let's pay The Right Honourable Carol James a visit."

## Chapter Seven

Number 13 Crompton Avenue was a large red brick property in mature gardens with electronic gates at the main entrance, a static camera on the right pillar focused on the gate and an intercom on the left-hand pillar. A high perimeter wall surrounded the property and, along the back garden, a line of trees hid the house and garden from the view of the street but then also hid the street from the house, leaving it wide open to a possible attack.

There was no sign of any roving security teams on the grounds and no other cameras at the property. While not quite amateur hour this was a more casual approach to home security of a high-profile figure like a Government Minister than Brannigan would have expected.

From a vantage point opposite, Brannigan and Chambers watched the grey Jaguar XKSS glide effortlessly through the electronic gates, crunching along the gravel driveway before coming to a halt outside the blue front door. Carol James got out of the back seat and on cue, the door of the house opened and the butler took a rather large and hideous-looking cloth bag along with a smart cream jacket from the Minister. Two agents got out of the car following behind the Jag and escorted her to the front door before peeling off left and right and patrolling the perimeter of the property. The front door closed and the Jag moved off to the garage at the side of the house. It looked like the Minister was home for the evening.

Brannigan and Chambers waited and counted. "Security takes two minutes to cover the house and grounds so we've got a minute thirty to get across the lawn and through that door," said Brannigan.

"How many people do you think we'll have to deal with?" asked Chambers.

"Hard to say. We know about the butler and the chauffeur. The two agents and the Minister make five, could be a personal assistant too, maybe a cook."

"So do you have a plan or are we just going to walk up and ring the bell?"

"Well, I was going to blow the Jag up, kill the guards and storm the house but I like your idea better."

Annette Chambers looked at him in disbelief.

"You're going to need this," he said and handed her Matt Jones' gun.

It always pays to know the strength of the opposition you're facing and Brannigan reckoned on six people plus the Minister. That wouldn't necessarily present a problem since only two of them were trained killers but then so were Brannigan and Chambers. The problem in this type of situation was the civilian; the have-a-go hero who invariably got you caught or killed. They relied exclusively on dumb luck and it was usually on their side.

So, the chauffeur, the butler, and maybe an assistant or a cook were the wild cards at play. The chauffeur was out of the way in the garage, the Butler wasn't exactly in the spring of youth so that left a possible personal assistant and a cook, who Brannigan hoped would be in the kitchen preparing the Minister's evening meal and safely out of the way.

They had the element of surprise and the best Ops were the ones where you get in and out quickly without anyone noticing or getting hurt. All they wanted to do was speak to Carol James and avoid the agents patrolling the grounds.

Basic camouflage gear of balaclava, trousers, and jacket from an army surplus store and face paints from the children's aisle of the local supermarket meant they were good to go. At just after 9 pm as the agents disappeared out of sight, they vaulted over the high wall and made their way along the grass verge of the driveway and pushed the doorbell.

Time ticked by while they waited for the butler to answer the door. After 90 excruciating seconds the front door opened. Brannigan moved in first, Glock held shoulder high and tight to the chest pointing straight at the butler's head. A raised index finger to his lips and the butler stayed quiet. Annette Chambers quickly followed and closed the door gently behind her as the gravel crunched outside.

The hall was large with a central staircase leading up to the first-floor mezzanine off which there were two corridors, one on each side. Portraits adorned the walls on the ground floor. There were two doors on the right and another three on the left. One of the doors on the left was marked 'study'. A corridor behind the stairs led to the kitchen and possibly the garden beyond.

"Where's Ms. James?" said Brannigan quietly.

The butler didn't answer but a brief, involuntarily flicker of his eyes toward the study gave him away. There was no sign of any other staff in this part of the house. The butler was coshed with the butt of the Glock and left unconscious against the front door as a doorstop against any unwelcome guests.

Carol James sat behind a large wooden desk attending to some papers, she looked up, startled when Brannigan entered the room and instinctively reached for the panic button on the left-hand side of the desk. "I wouldn't!" demanded Brannigan "Relax and live"

Ms. James relaxed back into her red leather chair and stared calmly at the intruders. This woman didn't frighten easily. Up close Brannigan could see the resemblance to the portraits hanging in the hallway. Carol James came from old money.

This room was smaller than he expected, cosy almost, lit by the little lamp on her desk. Bookshelves filled three of the walls from floor to ceiling and on the back wall heavy curtains hung over what appeared to be French Doors leading to the garden. Annette Chambers joined Brannigan in the middle of the room.

"My name is..." began Brannigan

"I know your name, your face is all over the news, what I don't know is why you're here?" interrupted the Minister, she almost spat the words out.

"I want justice for my friends" he continued, but it sounded lame as soon as he had said it. What he really meant was he wanted revenge.

Carol James sensed his dilemma. "There is no justice to be had here Mr. Brannigan because there is no law anymore, not in the true sense of the word anyway. It's all about manipulation and control in every country, everywhere. Do you know anything about Neo-Democracy, Mr. Brannigan?"

"I've heard of it, it's about creating a new independent UK," was all he said.

"Oh but it's so much more than that!" There was excitement in her voice. "You see leaving the EU is part of a global strategy Mr. Brannigan, a strategy that began soon after the Second World War to ensure control of the world's population and prevent the rise of another world power like the Third Reich.. We have been working on this for a very long time and now we have people in key positions of influence and power all over the world."

"The European Union was designed to be part of this and the introduction of the Euro was to help establish the United States of Europe, but they got greedy and we realised we had to get out. All this posturing in the news is just window dressing for the people. We had to make sure of the result of course which wasn't difficult. I told you we have people everywhere."

"We have elections, referendums, and laws of sorts but none of it matters. I mean if you're building a spaceship to take us to Mars would you ask the opinion of a shop worker or hairdresser? Of course not! So why would you ask people their opinion on matters they know nothing about?"

This was all very interesting until he noticed a tiny red light flashing on her right wrist. "Shit, she's stalling. She called for help!" shouted Brannigan.

"You should have disappeared when you had the chance, MISTER Brannigan."

A loud bang brought the conversation to an end. The front door was blown off its hinges and the butler died instantly. Armed officers swarmed into the house and Brannigan swung around to find Annette Chambers pointing her gun at him.

"I thought you were my best chance of staying alive, maybe I was wrong," and she shot Carol James, Secretary of State for Exiting the European Union right between the eyes. "I liked Sir Alistair," was all she managed to say before the library door was kicked open and tear gas lobbed into the room.

Instinctively Brannigan smashed through the French doors and ran across the back lawn toward the trees and the road beyond. Behind him he heard the unmistakable sound of the semi-automatic MPS Carbine, a favourite of the Metropolitan Police.

A blazing pain ripped through his shoulder as the first bullet struck, he stumbled forward but kept going. The second bullet hit him lower down the body, just at the top of the thigh, causing him to stumble further forward, head down like a drunken man out of control. He kept going before crashing headlong into the long grass at the edge of the garden. He scrambled in amongst the trees and over the wall onto the road.

He had come out quite a bit down from the electronic gates; they were now wide open, flashing lights from the driveway filling the night sky as he made his way down the road and into the darkness.

He was bleeding heavily and needed medical attention. He knew his blood pressure would drop and he would lose consciousness soon, but he had to hide the Carter file. The belt of his trousers provided a tourniquet for his leg, cutting off the blood flow from the femoral artery. He shoved his balaclava under his jacket and into the exit wound in his shoulder and he moved as fast as he could down the street.

In the garden of the house at the far end of Compton Avenue, he noticed a tree that looked out of place among the row of elms; it was smaller than the others and bushier, some sort of Maple he thought. He rammed the file into the centre of this little tree before heading toward the bright lights and the sound of people having fun.

He found himself in a square, with bars and restaurants wrapping themselves around the outside, tables, and chairs filling the centre. He heard someone scream as he fell to the ground and everything went dark.

**Day Five: The Chase**
**Chapter Eight**

Hearing is often the first sense to return as you regain consciousness and it was the beeping of the heart monitor that finally woke Jim Brannigan. He didn't know if he'd been out for a few minutes, a few hours, or a few days but he had heard the doctors and nurses talking. He knew that nurse Julie Raeburn was dating the new junior doctor, Dr. Carmichael. He had heard her laugh and joke with nurse Shreya Banik as only good friends can. He also heard them whispering about who he might be and why there were armed guards outside his room.

"What's this I hear about you and this new doctor Julie?"

"I'm sure I don't know what you mean Shreya."

"Now Julie, we all know that you and Doctor Carmichael are an item."

"You shouldn't listen to gossip Shreya, he's only here two minutes. He arrived just after our anonymous friend." Julie Raeburn nodded towards Brannigan.

"Yes, and what about Sleeping Beauty?" Shreya Banik lifted Brannigan's bed sheets and peeked under the cover.

"And he is a beauty!" Both Nurses laughed.

"You're incorrigible Nurse Banik."

"Who do you think he is Julie? Police at the door and him with two gunshot wounds and nothing on the TV or the radio. And no one in asking about him. No reporters, nothing"

"I guess there are some things we're better off not knowing Shreya. Now put his blanket down and let's go!"

Both nurses laughed and left the room. Brannigan lay with his eyes closed for a few minutes. He knew as soon as he opened them they'd all be in; the doctors, the nurses, the armed guards, and the others: the ones who put him in there in the first place. Still, he couldn't lie with his eyes closed forever so when the corridor went quiet he blinked as light streamed into his optic nerve and he squinted slightly to ease the pain.

It took a few seconds to focus on the room; the monitors beeping, the curtains covering the windows, the television on the wall showing a news channel in silence, and a few more seconds to feel the handcuffs clamping his right hand to the bed. On the plus side, he wasn't dead which meant they didn't want him dead, yet which meant they hadn't found the file.

He struggled to sit up as Nurse Raeburn re-entered the room. "Oh, I see you're awake!"

She busied herself checking monitors and puffing up pillows "Let's see if we can get you to sit up a little, shall we?" She said it like it was some sort of test, perhaps it was. "Wait, how long have you been awake?"

"Long enough to know I'm a beauty apparently." smiled Brannigan.

"Ah, I see. Ah, sorry about that. Doctor Carmichael will want a word, I'll just go and get him. Sorry, again, but I'll have to tell the police as well."

A picture of Annette Chambers popped up on the TV screen above the heading 'Breaking News'. Brannigan lifted the TV remote control and turned up the volume.

*It's just been released that the person responsible for the murder of The Right Honourable Carol James MP at her home in London last night was Annette Chambers. Ms. Chambers was also responsible for the death of Sir Alistair McIntyre, a retired banker with connections to the Conservative Party, at Vauxhall Tube Station early yesterday morning. The Metropolitan Police have confirmed that Ms. Chambers was a known radical and a supporter of the remain campaign to keep the United Kingdom in the EU. Her GP, Dr. Hillary Banks, has issued a statement saying that Annette Chambers had been suffering from*

*depression lately and had been in the care of a psychiatrist for some time. It is reported that she had become fixated with the Minister and her staff and her recent internet activity included searches for Carol James' home address. The Metropolitan Police say it appears she acted alone and they are not looking for anyone else in connection with the murder.*
*Ms. Chambers' father, Professor Mike Chambers of Oxford University has, however, rejected these claims and is demanding a full public inquiry into the shooting. The Home Office say they have no plans to hold such an inquiry at this time. In other news...."*

Brannigan turned the volume down as the door opened.

It wasn't Dr. Carmichael or the police who came through the door, it was Susan. She was carrying a small plastic carrier bag and she looked like she hadn't slept in days. Her eyes were sunken, with dark rings around the sockets, her hair was pulled back into a ponytail and lines dug deep across her face. They stared at one another, Brannigan's mouth was dry and he didn't know if he could speak, even if he knew what to say.

Susan sat down on the chair beside the bed. "They caught me on the way out the door. I should have left as soon as you phoned. I packed a bag turned off the gas, and left the house like I was going on holiday instead of running for my life". There were tears in her eyes now and she was looking down when she next spoke. "They threatened to torture me, Jim. Thought we were working together. They know I had been your analyst at ATU of course and reckoned we had some sort of big plan to bring down the Government or something.

They thought we were part of a network that John had set up."
Brannigan reached out and placed his hand on top of hers, she didn't pull away. "They want the file, Jim. They'll let us both go if you give it to them. We are to leave now, collect the file and bring it to ATU," she opened her hand to reveal a small key and unlocked the handcuffs. "Dr. Carmichael is to go with us along with Special Agent Jones, someone you know apparently? I don't think he's your biggest fan."

Susan emptied the contents of the carrier bag onto the bed; trainers, socks, black tracksuit bottoms and a blue sweat top. She helped him get dressed.
Dr. Carmichael came in. He was tall; maybe 6'3", about 180lbs and looked to be in good shape. "We're meeting Special Agent Jones in the hospital carpark. You two are to follow me." He turned to leave then stopped and turned

back to Brannigan "Oh, and if you try anything our orders are to kill Ms. Blakeshaw first."

They left the small private room and walked slowly down the corridor toward the lifts, Dr. Carmichael in front and two armed police officers at the rear. Brannigan thought this felt a little déjà vu. There was now no clear way out for either himself or Susan. If they got into the car with Matt Jones they were dead as soon as they handed over the Carter file, so whatever he was going to do he'd have to do it in the lift.

The carbines the police were carrying weren't made for close-range work. They were too bulky and if the police used them in the lift they'd probably kill everyone. He didn't know anything about Dr. Carmichael. He didn't even know if he was a Doctor, and even if he was he had to assume that he was an agent too so that made it three against one. Taking out your opponent's main weapon is always good advice, especially in a tight situation, so Dr. Carmichael was the prime target. Besides, the police relied on teamwork and a bit more space than a hospital lift for their training. Then there was Susan: an analyst not a field agent but a wild card that could get herself killed and maybe Brannigan too trying to save her.

The elevator doors swished open and Dr. Carmichael stepped inside followed by

Brannigan and Susan and the two officers entered last. Then they all did the lift shuffle, where everyone tries to find a little personal space and a spot on the wall to stare at. Brannigan made sure Susan was in front of him, facing the door. Carmichael was on his right-hand side, the two officers squashed together on his left. The elevator dropped quickly to the ground floor and the door swished open.

    Brannigan stretched his right hand out pointing toward the door and blocking Carmichael from leaving. "Ladies first". He stepped slightly aside to allow Susan to leave the elevator. Once she was outside he flicked his head back hard into Carmichael's face, breaking his second nose in as many days. He then stabbed the officer closest to him in the throat with the edge of his left hand, hard. The policeman's eyes widened and he gasped for breath as his windpipe collapsed. The second officer tried to raise his carbine, but the space was too tight. Brannigan smashed him in the mouth with his right fist as the door of the lift swished closed. He pushed the button for the roof. Carmichael was out cold and the policeman clawed at his throat in a vain attempt to avoid suffocation. The second policeman was choking on his own blood and teeth and as Cliff

Edwards sang 'When you wish upon a star' the lift ascended to the top of the building. Brannigan hauled the three unconscious bodies out onto the roof, took Carmichael's coat and ID badge and stepped back into the waiting elevator.

A few moments later the elevator door swished open once again on the ground floor and Brannigan stepped out wearing a somewhat bloodied doctor's coat and gently took an astonished Susan by the arm. They walked quickly out of the main doors of the hospital and into the bright summer sunshine, taking care to avoid the car park exit and the waiting Special Agent Jones.

## Chapter Nine

Special Agent Matt Jones sat in his black SUV with Agent Martin Johnson in the basement car park of St Bartholomew's Hospital waiting patiently for Dr. Carmichael and his entourage when his phone rang. "No sign of them yet," he replied. "I'll phone you when we're on our way." Matt Jones hung up and thought that maybe he sounded a little tetchy on the phone but then Special Agent Matt Jones was more than a little tetchy. Ever since he had his nose broken in the cube and was found unconscious in a pool of his own blood he had been mercilessly teased by his colleagues at ATU. He knew how to handle himself and when he got Jim Brannigan back to Vauxhall he'd prove that. Yes, Jim Brannigan was in a shitload of trouble and Matt Jones knew a thing or two about shovelling shit.

He was 35 years old for Christ's sake, most agents his age were either promoted or dead. Now he was being chastened by a twenty-something female and had his gun taken by an over-the-hill, ex-military dough head. Yes, it was fair to say Matt Jones was feeling a little tetchy today.

The interrogation rooms at ATU are below Vauxhall Tube Station; purposefully dark, dank, and inhospitable to friend and foe alike. They were built as service tunnels for the original underground railway in 1863 but had long been forgotten and now they had an altogether different use. The wailing of the desperate was drowned out by the thundering herds above.

Matt Jones grinned widely as he thought of the hours and days that lay ahead for former ATU Agent Jim Brannigan; a busted nose would be the least of his problems. He was deep in thought and hardly heard Agent Johnson speak.

"Who was that…Matt!?"

"Who do you think!?" was his curt reply.

"I heard she put you on the Combat Retraining Course."

"Yeah, I heard that too."

Both agents stared across the car park and towards the little lift in the far corner that led up to the main hospital entrance. It was Matt Jones who spoke first this time,

"I was with MI5 for Christ's sake!, swanning around Asia and the Middle East with a fucking expense account, working with the Chinese Intelligent Agency, flushing out terrorist training grounds. I was the fucking golden boy of the agency. Now I am stuck here with you."

Agent Johnson continued to stare out the window of the SUV and didn't appear to be too offended by that last remark.

"You did kill someone," he said eventually. "It wasn't someone, it was Atif Basheer. Intel confirmed he was Al-Qaeda so we blew him up with a roadside bomb."

"Except he wasn't, was he? He was an undercover CIA operative," replied Agent Johnston.

"Well, there is that."

His phone rang for a second time. "Yes, I'll go and hurry them up if you want…okay…. second floor…. yes, I'm armed…no, no, I don't need anyone to go with me." He was sure he detected a barely muffled snigger before the line went dead. "Fuck Sake!"

He had parked the SVU discreetly in bay C13 at the far end of the Hospital's underground car park. He had removed the overhead fluorescent strip lighting which kept the car in darkness and deterred any curious passers-by. He switched off the engine and took the keys, leaving Agent Jonson in complete darkness. "You wait here, I've to go babysit."

The elevator door opened onto the second floor, and hospital life buzzed around him like bees round honey. Machines beeped, flashed, and squeaked, people tapped keyboards or chatted over the water cooler. Everything seemed normal except there was no armed guard outside room 2C. He instinctively unclipped his gun from his shoulder holster. "Where's the patient from 2C?" he asked the tall receptionist with a rather pointed nose. Despite himself, he couldn't help but think she looked rather like a crow or a blackbird.

"Pardon?" said the crow, as she looked up from her screen and over the top of her glasses at Special Agent Jones.

"The patient in 2C, where is he?" Matt Jones was shouting now, drawing attention to himself.

"I really couldn't say," replied the receptionist, now in a bit of a fluster with everyone staring at her.

"He, ah…left here with that nice Dr. Carmichael and two officers a few minutes ago." Matt Jones quickly checked the rest of the floor before dialling in.

"No sign of anyone….no, I couldn't have missed them…. yes, I'm sure…..Lock down the hospital: Code Blue."

Brannigan and Blakeshaw dodged traffic as they ran across Heron Road and entered St Bartholomew's Charity shop opposite.

"Pick dark colours and make them baggy so they can't tell if you're a man or a woman," said Brannigan. "And get something with a hood if you can, or get a hat of some sort that covers your face a little. Meet me out back in the yard when you're done."

A few minutes later Susan Blakeshaw entered the backyard of the Charity shop dressed in baggy tracksuit bottoms and a baggy black hoodie and blue trainers. Brannigan was waiting, dressed in smart Jeans, a jacket and a baseball cap. Brown brogues completed a rather sharp look.

"The homeless look suits you."

"You should've seen the look the woman in the shop gave me when I came out of the changing room. Anyway, you said dark and baggy," replied Susan

"I know I did, but there are limits. Don't worry, we'll change a few more times on our way."

"On our way where?"

"The one place they won't look for us is John's apartment. We'll have to pick a few things up as we go."

They left the charity shop yard through the back gate and walked casually down the entry and onward to Carter's apartment.

Code Blue is just as serious as it sounds. It means the shit has just hit the fan and so everyone available descended on St Bartholomew's. Agents, clean-up squads, metropolitan police: in fact, just about anyone with a badge.

The brief was simple; get a cover story in place and find Jim Brannigan. TV trucks screeched to a halt outside St Bartholomew's Hospital and helicopters filled the London skies as perma-tanned reporters talked excitedly into cameras and microphones. They all fell silent for Mr. Brendan Maxwell, Chief Administrative Officer at St Bartholomew's.

"I can confirm that a radioactive leak occurred today at 10.45 am. The radioactive sensors on Corridor 1B which links the main hospital to the Radiation Therapy Wards recorded unusually high levels of radiation. As a precautionary measure, St Bartholomew's has been closed to the public. All ambulances have been redirected to the Royal London Hospital in Whitechapel and staff, patients, and visitors are being screened as a precaution. I would ask the public to please bear with us at this difficult time and I thank you for your understanding and patience. We are working closely with all the necessary agencies and I can assure you that due to the swift implementation of our biohazard protocol, there is no danger to the general public at this time. Further updates will be given throughout the day. Thank you."

Cameras flashed, and questions were fired like bullets at the Chief Administrative Officer, but Brendan Maxwell took no questions.

Inside the hospital, a systematic search was taking place of every room, cupboard and service elevator. Every nook and cranny in the entire building was double-searched for the two fugitives. Everyone that could be moved was brought to the public canteen for 'screening' and then on to the waiting buses for further processing at the local leisure centre before being released. Everyone else had their identity double-checked where they lay.

Special Agent Jones was certain there was no way out for Brannigan and Blakeshaw, that is until they found the bodies on the roof. A couple of nights later a junky with a gun would break into the hospital pharmacy, holding Dr. Carmichael hostage before killing the two officers who responded to the emergency call. He would appear to have killed Dr. Carmichael in a struggle before turning the gun on himself. Authorities would say that this regrettable incident was in no way connected to the radiation leak just a few days previously and their thoughts are with the families of the deceased at this time.

A black SVU weaved its way through the London traffic at speed and Matt Jones spoke frantically to his ATU analyst. "Contact Transport for London, tell them I need all eyes on St Bartholomew's Hospital and the surrounding area. I want every street camera, shop camera, bank machine camera, every fucking camera they have looking for Brannigan and Bradshaw. If they give you any shit, tell them I'm on my way to Windsor House right now and I better get what I fucking want!"

With over 500,000 cameras in London, Transport for London Headquarters at Windsor House was a good place to start looking for two needles in a rather large haystack. The odds of finding someone in London were no better than 50/50 despite Londoners being caught on camera an average of seventy times each day.

These images are mostly taken at work or on shop front CCTV cameras. If you live or work in one of the 'hot spots' areas of the city you could be captured on camera up to three hundred times a day. That's millions of faces on thousands of cameras hundreds of times every day. Even with facial recognition software you still need a lot of luck to pick someone out of the crowd. Knowing their last location and time of day helps narrow the search field but you still need that bit of luck. Once you have them you can track their every move from camera to camera.

Matt Jones was hoping Brannigan and Blakeshaw would turn up sooner rather than later. He was feeling lucky after all.

## Chapter Ten

"Any sign of them?"

A long painted fingernail tapped repeatedly on the green leather top of a boardroom table. "We need to get that file back and find Carter's laptop. It's worse than we thought; Carter hacked the Echelon Satellite Security System and changed the command code. He's locked us out of our own system! We think the new command code will be on his laptop so whoever has the laptop has control of the United Kingdom's global Anti-Terrorist network."

With so much at stake, not least of all her own life, Annette Chambers was getting somewhat impatient. She set her phone down but immediately picked it up again and rang back. "Go and hurry them up…. they're on the second floor…. are you armed?" Despite herself, she couldn't suppress a quiet little snigger as she heard Matt Jones sigh on the other end of the phone.

Matt Jones was a friend of sorts and she almost felt sorry for him, but he was the lead agent when Brannigan escaped from ATU headquarters and so it was his fault that McIntyre was dead.

They had met on her first day at ATU, she had transferred across from GCHQ and he was just back from Asia. Her career was moving upwards while his was in the shitter, something about a dead American agent she seemed to recall. No doubt about it, Matt Jones' best days were behind him.

Sometimes quick decisions have to be made and Annette Chambers wasn't afraid of making a quick decision or two. She knew one day that approach could get her in trouble, but not this day. Killing Sir Alistair and escaping with Brannigan kept the trail alive. Brannigan was their best hope of getting Carter's laptop she was sure of it. This was her plan and if it failed so did she: no wonder then that Annette Chambers was getting a little impatient.

She was pondering her next move when her phone buzzed gently and shimmied along the table.

"Could you have missed them...are you sure...okay, consider Bartholomew's locked down." She hung up and slammed her phone down hard on the green leather tabletop, "Shit!"

She lifted the receiver of the secure landline in the boardroom. "Code Blue at St Bartholomew's, alert our friends in the media before any of this gets out and add Susan Blakeshaw to the terrorist watch list. Issue a press release on her through the usual channels telling the public she was the Intelligence Officer for the cell responsible for the murders of the Chinese Delegates in Edinburgh and the recent London bombing. She is to be considered armed and dangerous and must not be approached. Oh, and tell the security services to shoot her on sight."

She sat back and contemplated her next move. Maybe every cloud does have a silver lining after all.

"Ms. Chambers, they're ready for you." She was brought out of her daydream by the sight and sound of Gabriella Santini's head popped around the now open door of the boardroom. The head was about six feet off the ground and with no visible signs of support looked simply surreal. Gabriella smiled her best business smile and waited for a response. None was forthcoming, and her head withdrew from the room and was followed by the sound of high heels click-clacking into the distance.

Annette got up and followed the sound down the corridor to a small office where Ms. Santini now sat bolt upright behind a well-kept desk. Her dark hair in curls down to her waist, she wore a smart blue striped business suit and looked suitably busy on her computer. She did not glance up as Annette Chambers walked passed and stood before the door to the inner office.

An eye scanner on the wall confirmed her identity and she entered perhaps the most important room in the whole of the United Kingdom. She sat in the only chair in the middle of a small room and faced a bank of screens that covered the entire wall. The screens were filled with images of similar rooms from all over the world. There was Australia, Canada, New Zealand, the United States of America, France, Russia and Germany. Annette Chambers had a seat at the big table and she wasn't about to give it up for anyone.

"The first order of business is a roundup of key activities and strategies," It was New Zealand that spoke. "As chair of this session I will report last and since we have a new representative from the United Kingdom I suggest we start there, unless anyone has any objections?" There were no objections so after a short pause she continued, "Ms. Chambers would you care to update us on recent developments:"

"Yes, well…of course" began Annette Chambers somewhat hesitantly. She shuffled papers and continued nervously "This quarter the UK is working with partner countries to reduce farming standards and allow the introduction of GM foods and hormones into beef production as planned; we continue to undermine the National Health Service in the media to create opportunities for external Healthcare Corporations as per our undertaking in 2017. Let me see…yes, our work on restricting India's ability to produce affordable medicines should be completed post Brexit, ensuring the control of world pharmaceuticals should pass to us within months of any trade deal"

"Yes, that's all very interesting," interrupted New Zealand. "But I was thinking more about the mess you're in with leaked Brexit referendum results and missing satellite codes.".

Annette Chambers began to feel the sweat run down the back of her neck. It sure was warm at the big table.

## Chapter Eleven

On King Edward Street Brannigan and Blakeshaw avoided the Pedestrian Crossing and the PTZ surveillance cameras hidden within the red stop lights. Their biggest problem now was to avoid as many of the surveillance cameras as possible so there would be no walking past security gates, ATMs or anything in need of 24-hour protection.

Police cameras on the other hand are trickier as they are designed to cover large crowds and have zoom capability, but they operate from a height so a cap or a hood can be employed to shield your face as would simply looking down as much as possible. Of course, randomly altering your appearance is advisable so Brannigan and Blakeshaw needed to look for shops with no CCTV coverage and charity shops were usually a good bet.

All of which was why, even though John Carter's apartment was only a few minutes' walk from the hospital, it took them over an hour to make it to the Fishmonger's Café opposite the apartment block. On the way, they picked up a laser-light pen and ten little Infrared LEDs from a department store on the corner of Westferry Road.

Now they sat outside the café, wrapped up against the evening cold, and waited for dark. Two coffees sat untouched and a small plastic bag lay on the table. Susan put her hand into the bag and pulled out one of the little LED lights.

"So, what are these things for?"

"They'll knock out the cameras on the front door of the apartment block for a few seconds, nothing but white light while we enter the building. If anyone should check, it will be a glitch in the system, nothing more."

"And the little pen thing?"

"It does the same thing really, it's backup."

Brannigan scanned the early evening crowds for any sign of surveillance. He couldn't see anything or anyone suspicious. "You ready?" Susan nodded "Then, grab the bag, and let's go"

Susan scattered a couple of the LEDs onto the steps of the apartment as they approached and they entered the building without a hitch. On the fourth floor, everything was quiet. Brannigan reckoned they'd be safe here till morning at least, time to rest and make a plan of escape. He was sure no one had followed them…until there was a knock on the front door. He signalled to Susan to move down the corridor and into one of the bedrooms. There was no point switching off the lights and hiding but he wasn't about to stand in front of the door and look through the peephole either in case he got a 22-caliber bullet in his brain.

"Hold on" he shouted, "With you in a sec!". He crouched down, reached up to the lock, and gingerly opened the door a crack to see a middle-aged woman standing outside number 35A. She was wearing a nightgown and some rather ridiculous pink fluffy slippers, and she was holding a package. "Hello, May I help you?" he said in a rather too jolly and slightly idiotic voice as he stood up.

"Well.... yes, I think so. I'm Mrs Gorman your next-door neighbour. Well, not YOUR next-door neighbour but dear Mr. Carter's next-door neighbour. This package came for him but it was addressed to MY apartment and I don't know what to do with it, especially after that dreadful business in Edinburgh. I was going to give it to the postman tomorrow but then I heard noises and thought maybe that nice girl of his had come back."

"I could take it if you like? Leave it here for Annette, Mr. Carter's girlfriend?" said Brannigan helpfully.

"Well, I don't know...... they're always telling us to report anything suspicious," said Mrs. Gorman, as much to herself as to Brannigan.

Brannigan's patience was growing thin; he thought if he had his gun he might just shoot her, take the damn package and dump her body where she'd never be found. He decided against that particular course of action.

"I know, you can never be too careful. I never open the door to strangers but then you're not a stranger. You're the lovely lady from next door aren't you?"

"Well yes! That's what I said, that's me, Mrs. Gorman from next door!" Mrs. Gorman shuffled slightly and looked a little uncomfortable now. "I'm sure it'll be alright," she said eventually, "you look like such a nice young man" and she handed over the package. "Thank you," he said and smiled his widest smile before gently closing the door on Mrs. Gorman.

"All clear" he said to Susan.

"What is it?" she asked "Well John sent it to himself. See those little circles above the 'i's, they were something of a trademark of his in the army."

"I'll give you three guesses but you'll only need one."

"John's laptop" replied Susan.

Brannigan set the package on the coffee table, took the silver laptop out, and lifted the screen. The machine sprang into life, bleeping and tinkling its way to the start-up page and the password request box.

"Any ideas about a password?" he asked. "Not really, I know nothing about John," Susan replied.

"We could try and reach someone through the dark web, maybe put a shout-out on Alphabay or Hansa? Try and get someone to hack the laptop and tell us what's on it that's so important? What made John send it to himself?"

"That might work," said Brannigan "For now, let's get some rest, I've a feeling tomorrow's going to be a long and difficult day for both of us."

The adrenalin rush of the last few hours was wearing off and tiredness invaded them both.

"I'm hungry. I assume pizza is out of the question?" Susan asked hopefully.

Brannigan's expression gave her the answer. There was no food in Carter's apartment and they couldn't risk raising suspicion by passing the front door cameras again or ordering takeaway food so they sat on the couch, lost in their own thoughts and in silence.

"Well, if I can't eat at least I can shower," said Susan eventually. She leaned forward and kissed Brannigan on the forehead.

It wasn't long before he could hear her singing softly above the rush of the water and tiredness bore into him.

He followed her down the corridor a few minutes later. The bathroom door was ajar and he couldn't help a glance to see Susan with her back to the door slowly, almost sensually, washing. Her smooth skin and perfect shape reminded him of Jennifer and Brannigan's heart ached for all that he had lost. He felt like a voyeur invading someone's private moment and yet he was transfixed by longing and desire.

Susan stepped out of the shower and turned around to find herself alone, the bathroom door ajar and the corridor empty. She knew he had been watching her; she had left the door open for him. She had felt his eyes upon her; she wanted him to see her, to desire her. She wanted the feel of him inside her, making love to her like she imagined he made love to Jennifer. She reached for the dressing gown hanging up behind the door and wrapped it tightly around her.

On a big screen in Windsor House Special Agent Matt Jones watched two people enter John Carter's Apartment block. A flash of light blinded the camera on the steps for a few seconds but the street camera across the road was still recording. Matt Jones picked up his radio. "Commander, I've found them; they're in Carter's apartment! I need full tactical assault support." A satellite image of the area showed the nearest landing site to be waste ground at North 51.30.33/West 01.18. 02. "Rendezvous in 20 minutes and don't do anything 'till I get there," Matt Jones ran from Windsor House. He wanted to be the one who retrieved the Carter file and the codes but more than that he wanted Jim Brannigan. Damn right it was personal and if he hurried he could beat the rush hour traffic.

Meanwhile, schematics of the building were being sent to Adam Chance, Commander of ATU's Special Forces Unit. The nature of the assault on the building would be his decision and he didn't answer to Matt Jones, he answered to the new Director of ATU. Commander Chance looked at Annette Chambers. "What do you want me to do?"

"Get over there ahead of Jones, secure the laptop"

"How do you know he has the laptop?" asked Commander Chance.

"He has the laptop."

"And Special Agent Jones?"

"I'll take care of Matt Jones, and leave no witnesses," was the blunt reply.

"Give me an update Commander, I'm mobile and will be with you in fifteen minutes."

Matt Jones sounded calm and in control, but he was buzzing with excitement and looking forward to his meeting with Jim Brannigan.

"I've sent a two-man team to set a small explosive device in the basement to blow all power and communications in the building. I have a five-man snatch squad in a van opposite the building dressed as Metropolitan Police Officers and I've got a prep squad from the 'gas board' going door to door to clear the bottom 3 floors, leaving just the top floor and our suspects. There may be casualties, but they'll be within acceptable levels, we should be good to go in 5-10 minutes." replied Commander Chance.

"I said wait till I get there, I'm the lead agent on this and you'll do as you're told, is that clear?" But Commander Chance wasn't listening.

Matt Jones had now joined the thousands of commuters snaking their way home along busy London streets but there were others, others he didn't know who were making their way to St George's Wharf.

It was the tremble of the building that Brannigan felt first, then the build-up of pressure in his ears before the windows of the apartment shattered and glass filled the air. Smoke and dust choked every room. Brannigan moved low and fast up the corridor checking for Susan as he went; he found her dazed but conscious on the floor of the living room. He helped her to her feet and swiped the laptop off the table. In the hallway, the stairs leading down to the ground floor bellowed smoke and flames and a dragon's roar echoed around the entire building. Going down didn't seem like an option.

"We have to get out of here!" he shouted. "We have to go up!" They climbed the stairs two at a time, Brannigan in front almost dragging Susan along behind him.

"Come on!" he shouted, "You have to keep up!" It was exhausting climbing the stairs, the heat and dust pressed into them, squeezing the life out. They were nearly at the top, scrambling past others on their hands and knees who would never make it. Sirens howled on the streets below as Brannigan crashed through the door and onto the roof.

There were a few other people there already "What do you think, a gas explosion?" asked Susan.

"We're under attack!" shouted Brannigan, "We have to get off this roof. Somehow they've found us."

"But how!?" cried Susan.

"Damned if I know!"

Susan hardly reacted as the bullet ripped through her right shoulder. Just a slight stiffening of her upper body before slumping forward, blood pooling beneath her. Brannigan dived away from the open door as radios crackled "The female is down, repeat the female is down."

He had no weapon and no chance of escape; police in body armour swarmed up the stairs and spilled out onto the roof just as the helicopter came into view. The blast from the smoke bomb surprised the officers and they retreated into the relative safety of the stairwell. People scattered in panic.

The helicopter hovered just above the rooftop and the side door slid open. The invitation was obvious and Brannigan didn't refuse. He sprinted to the helicopter and threw himself inside. He rose high above the building, high above the skyline, and high above Susan.

## Chapter Twelve

"Tracker Niner-Seven-Three-Juliet-Charlie-One has been activated. I repeat, Tracker Niner-Seven-Three-Juliet-Charlie-One has been activated. The target location is Aquarius House, fourth floor, apartment 35A, St George's Wharf, London SE24. I say again, the location is…"

Alisa Petrov didn't need to hear the location again and that wasn't just because she knew London as well as she knew her hometown of St Petersburg. It was because she already knew that particular address very well indeed.

Within minutes of receiving the message on her Non-Terrestrial Mobile Radio Device, or NMR phone for short, Alisa Petrov had left the Russian Embassy in Kensington Palace Gardens. She pulled out into the early evening traffic when the explosion occurred. It was loud enough to be heard all over the city and within seconds the drive-time radio show was interrupted with news reports of a gas explosion at St George's Wharf.

*"Casualties are unknown but a terrorist attack was not suspected at this time,"* the announcer said. *"Members of the public are being asked to avoid the area if at all possible, and major delays are expected across the city*

*this evening. Emergency services are at the scene and the Metropolitan Police are putting a one-mile perimeter in place as a precaution. A further update will be given in our main news bulletin at eight o'clock. In the meantime its back to Ed Sheeran and Galway Girl"*

With London now gridlocked she abandoned her car in the nearest side street and made her way on foot toward St George's Warf and Carter's laptop.

Although she didn't know which branch, it was obvious to Alisa Petrov that British Security Services were using the gas explosion story as cover. It did seem quite extreme to blow up an entire building in an attempt to recover a laptop. Unless there was another reason. Unless they wanted the laptop destroyed and everyone who knew about it dead. Then an explosion made perfect sense, hide one event inside another, bigger event. Perfect misdirection and perfect fake news.

Alisa knew this world very well, for although her work visa gave her status as a translator for the Russian Government, she was a Cyber Terror Specialist. Her real job was to cause confusion and chaos to computer systems all over the world to benefit or progress Russian interests. Her specialty was fake news stories across the internet, stories that could help elect presidents or topple governments but mainly anything that promoted Russian interests was within her brief and London was one of the biggest centres for fake news in the world.

She worked as part of a large team, each person responsible for their own thread of fake news and discord. Her current assignment was to create fake news stories that would mislead the British Government into thinking they would have direct trade links with Russia once they exited the EU. This 'misunderstanding' would ultimately undermine the British economy and create a financial crisis. Anything that impacted Western capabilities was good for Russia.

It was through this assignment that she first met John Carter, when rumours surfaced that he was disgruntled and a potential Government whistleblower. They got to know each other, and he trusted her, and they were lovers for a while. He confided in her about his misgivings about his work at ATU and the long-term goals of the Global Intelligence Alliance but she had no such misgivings. She thought Carter a fool and played him for one. Now all she wanted was the laptop and the codes that were locked away inside it.

"The target is on the move, I say again, the target is on the move and appears to be heading for the roof." The voice in her earpiece crackled into life. They were getting real-time updates from the tracker in the laptop and whoever had the device was most likely heading for the roof in the hope of finding a way of escape.

She'd never make it to St George's Wharf in time and if the target was running then they were being chased. She was a CST agent and would be of no use in that sort of situation. She was no field agent after all and she could very likely get herself killed. Something she wasn't planning on happening anytime soon.

"We'll need aerial support to the roof immediately." She spoke quietly and quickly into her phone "British Security Services will be in hard pursuit of the target. Divert one of our media helicopters to the location and tell them no casualties, smoke grenades only. Secure the device and meet me at the Battersea Heliport."

Alisa Petrov changed direction and headed toward the Thames, and the River Bus that would take her to the Heliport. She sat impatiently on the River Bus contemplating her next move. She knew with the laptop would come the codes and with the codes would come an opportunity to flood the United Kingdom's worldwide surveillance network with fake news. Her time with John Carter had been well spent; she had become part of his 'Global Hackers

Alliance,' as he liked to call his little team. A bunch of dropouts and misfits thought Alisa, although there was no doubting their skill.

The boat reached the Helipad just as the helicopter touched down, and the reporter from KYB news jumped out with Brannigan close behind. If Alisa was surprised to see him she hid it well.

"Follow me," she shouted above the noise of the chopper's blades. Brannigan followed but the reporter climbed back into the helicopter and took off across the city, back to Canary Wharf.

"My name's Alisa Petrov, I was a friend of John Carter's," she said quietly once they had entered the helipad reception area. Brannigan looked at her but didn't say anything. Alisa pressed on. "I'm part of John's team, not ATU, his other team." Brannigan nodded as though he knew what she was talking about and guessed this would be the team that Susan had mentioned.

"John put a tracker in the laptop; it was activated as soon as you opened it. The problem is we're not the only ones tracking it. Whoever blew up the apartment knows you have it, we need to get out of here"

"What about Susan?" asked Brannigan "The woman who was with me on the roof, the one who was shot?"

"I don't know, I'll contact the helicopter, now let's go!" She turned and walked outside to a waiting car. In the absence of a better plan, Brannigan followed her. Alisa got into the front passenger seat and Brannigan got in the back. Alisa opened the glove box taking out what looked like a little in-car cigarette lighter with a little rubber antenna attached. She plugged it in and the GPS jamming device flashed green. "They won't be able to track you with this little beauty on our side." The car sped off, heading north out of London, away from ATU and away from Susan.

Alisa Petrov's earpiece crackled into life once more and she turned to Brannigan. "Susan's alive; our news team has confirmed she was loaded into an ambulance a few minutes ago."

"Then we should go back" said Brannigan. He knew the hospital was the best place for Susan but he was testing this new friendship with Alisa Petrov.

"Absolutely not," replied Alisa softly. "Our best bet is to get this laptop open and secure the codes. Once we have them then we can bargain for her life."

"What codes?" asked Brannigan.

Alisa looked at him with total surprise and laughed. "You don't know what's on that laptop, do you? You've no idea what this is all about or how much trouble you're in?"

"All I know is that for the last few days I've been shot, blown up and chased all over the UK, two of my friends are dead, another is shot and now I'm in a car with two Russian agents. Why don't you tell me about the codes?" He knew a little more than that of course but it would do him no good to reveal anything more at this point. Besides he didn't like Alisa Petrov and he certainly didn't trust her.

"It's all about control, Mr. Brannigan. You know that the Echelon Satellite is a Surveillance System, the most advanced spy system in the world. It is so advanced that it can monitor billions of communications daily, search for keywords or phrases and attack any computer network in the world. It was most recently used to disable North Korea's nuclear launch programme but has capabilities far beyond that. The satellite was under the control of the Americans and the British as part of their 'special relationship' you hear so about in the media. That is until John Carter hacked the system, changed the codes and locked them out. But this 'special relationship' is just media spin for the Community Intelligence Agreement of 1945 and the setting up of the Five Eyes Project."

"No telling what the system could do in the wrong hands," said Brannigan sarcastically.

"Exactly!" replied Alisa "That's why John and I formed our little group. He called us the *Global Hackers' Alliance*. We have to get the satellite codes and destroy Echelon as John wanted."

"And how big is this team?"

"There are only four of us and we're on our way to meet the rest of them now as it happens. I'm not a Russian agent by the way. I'm a translator for the Russian Embassy in London but I too want the same things John did, an end to the manipulation of world events for financial gain. That's why I became part of his team."

Brannigan sensed he was still being played but for now she was probably right about one thing; he could trade the codes for Susan's life and if Alisa got in the way then she would forfeit hers.

He stared out the window of the speeding vehicle as motorway signs for Edinburgh flashed by: it seemed he was going there after all. He closed his eyes and replayed the events of the last few hours. Alisa Petrov and the driver spoke softly in Russian and although Brannigan couldn't have known it, orders had come through to keep him alive, at least for the time being. Tiredness once again overtook him and he slept. Eventually, the car slowed and the familiar hum of Motorway driving gave way to the unmistakable noise of rush hour traffic.

He opened his eyes as they slowed further and entered the Clock Tower Industrial Estate a few miles south of Edinburgh. The driver pulled up outside a disused warehouse at the far end of the estate. The door in the roller shutter opened and a rather gawky teenager ambled toward the car and joined Brannigan in the back seat. He looked at Alisa: "Is that it?" She nodded and he reached for the laptop only to receive a smack across the face for his trouble.

"What the fuck!" He glared at Brannigan as blood dripped from his nose. He dabbed it with his finger then held his hand out and inspected it curiously as though it belonged to someone else. "What you do that for?" he mumbled.

"You touch that laptop again and I'm liable not to act so reasonably next time," said Brannigan

"Now Jim, may I call you Jim?" asked Alisa. Without waiting for a reply she continued. "Alex here was only going to attach a little magnetic mobile GPS jammer to the laptop. It's just like the one we have in the car. After all, we wouldn't want anyone to find you now would we?"

Brannigan didn't like the way she said that but he nodded to Alex who slapped the jamming device onto the top of the laptop and muttered something about a 'fucking bastard' which Brannigan thought just might have been directed at him. He let it pass.

The inside of the warehouse was empty and dark, the only light coming from a small skylight in the roof. Four concrete walls encased a five-meter square concrete floor. There was an emergency exit door in the far right corner of the back wall and to the left a set of stairs leading to three small rooms above.

The warehouse might have looked vacant to the casual observer except for a faint glow coming from under the door of the last room, the sort of glow a television set or computer screen might make. This little merry band made their way up the stairs and along to room three. The driver stayed with the car.

Alisa punched a code into a keypad on the wall outside the room and pushed gently on the door.

Inside were two people whom she introduced as Charlie and Noel. They nodded but didn't look up from the computer screen in front of them which was showing images from five little rooms, and beneath each one was the name of a country. Brannigan recognised them as the countries of the Five Eyes Project. He also recognised a tall woman in her late twenties. She had an almost Caribbean complexion and although he couldn't see the colour of her eyes he suspected they would be deep blue; Annette Chambers was alive and well and sitting in a room marked 'United Kingdom'.

"You got any sound in those rooms?" He directed the question to either Charlie or Noel but it was Alex who answered

"Nah, we've just managed to hack into some achieved files from the TAO. These are days old and there's no audio"

"TAO?" asked Brannigan. Charlie or Noel sniggered, and Brannigan could feel his temper rising. Alex wasn't the only one who might get a smack in the mouth today.

"It stands for Tailored Access Operations," said Alisa "It's part of the American Intelligence Network: comes under NSA but is secretive, a bit like their version of ATU except when they arrest hackers they usually employ them to hack into other countries' systems not jail them like you Brits.

They currently work as part of the Joint Forces Cyber Group here in the UK. In Vauxhall to be precise, in a building I think you know very well. This is a very complicated business Jim, VERY COMPLICATED." She said the last two words very slowly like she was talking to a small child. Another candidate for a smack in the mouth thought Brannigan.

"Right, let's get this baby cracked open said Alex a little bit too enthusiastically but no one else seemed to notice.

Brannigan put the laptop on the empty table facing the door and opened it, once again the machine sprang into life, beeping and tinkling its way to the start-up page. Alex plugged what looked like his own smaller laptop into it. "The password is stored in the computer so I'm loading up a program that will allow me access as an Administrator and I should be able to recover the password. I wrote the program myself." He might have been talking to Brannigan but mostly he seemed to be talking to himself and he smiled widely at the knowledge, but once again no one seemed to notice.

It didn't take long before he got a ping. He was over the first hurdle and the main screen now contained a series of folders each one password protected and only identifiable by a 4-digit number. Alex was confident that he could open them all and get Carter's laptop to give up its secrets.... eventually.

The high expectation of the first few minutes gave way to a degree of impatience that in turn give way to boredom as minutes turned into hours. File after file was opened and while mildly interesting to someone like John Carter they contained mostly staff appraisal forms and diary appointment notes. Brannigan sat in a chair in the corner and sighed. "If you people hacked the system why don't you already have the codes?"

It seemed a reasonable enough question, but someone sniggered. It was Charlie who spoke this time or maybe it was Noel, Brannigan didn't know which was which. "We all worked on different aspects of the hacking process and only John had sight of all the different pieces of the jigsaw. He figured out the sequence of the code that would unlock Echelon." He said it so matter of factly that Brannigan now felt stupid for asking. He had another question, but he thought he'd keep it to himself for the time being.

Of course, as the way with these things, it was the last-but-one folder that contained the start-up codes for Echelon. "Eureka!" shouted Alex "We have the code." He plugged in a USB stick and downloaded the file just as his face splashed across the screen of the exploding laptop. Charlie and Noel looked in horror at the last thing they would ever see before their heads exploded. Alisa Petrov pointed her Glock 42 at Brannigan.

It's strange what goes through one's mind at a time of stress. In Brannigan's case it was the G42 that Petrov held in her hand. This is the smallest and lightest of the Glock range. Ideal for pocket carry and with six ACP rounds it was an ideal weapon in a tight situation.

"Someone wants you alive; otherwise you'd be joining these dopes. Can't understand why, you're as dumb as shit. Now give me that USB. And wipe it clean first"
She was right, he had been dumb; dumb to climb the stairs when he knew there was no way out, dumb to trust her. He'd been dumb about a lot of things, but he was tired of being dumb.

He pulled the USB out of the now destroyed laptop. It was soaked in Alex's blood and tissue so it only took a little squeeze for it to plop onto the floor in front of him. For a split second Alisa looked down and Brannigan did what he had wanted to do all day. He hit her an almighty smack in the mouth with the back of his left hand, and while she was stunned he followed through with a right-handed punch square on the face that propelled her backward off her feet causing her to smash into the door. She crumpled to the ground and he pulled the

Glock from her hand and shoved it into his belt. He grabbed her by the neck and tilted her head upward, ready to land another blow but she was already unconscious and bleeding badly. He let go of her and she flopped to the ground like a rag doll. He shoved her out of the way, picked up the USB and exited the warehouse through the back door.

    He was running now, adrenalin pumping through his body. He felt alive, excited even. He knew Susan was alive and he knew Annette Chambers was alive and he had the Echelon codes. Now, if he could stay alive long enough he could trade those codes and the Carter file for Susan's life. All he had to do was get in touch with Annette Chambers and pay a visit to a certain little tree in Crompton Avenue.

## Chapter Thirteen

Matt Jones parked his SUV and walked the remaining distance to the rendezvous point. He couldn't wait to remind Adam Chance who was in charge of this operation. He was almost at the van when the whole street seemed to shake, and the apartment block exploded in front of him; smoke and glass rained down on screaming Londoners as the doors of the van burst open and the assault team charged into the building. Outside people were running and screaming in all directions. Emergency Rapid Response Teams could already be heard wailing their way to the scene of the explosion and all Matt Jones could do was quickly melt into the crowds.

Body Cams were on and Commander Chance watched his team move into the building and up to the fourth floor; apartment 35A was empty and the squad moved up the stairs toward the roof. The point man spotted Brannigan ahead of them practically dragging a woman along behind him. He managed to burst through the door onto the roof as the point man fired a single shot and the woman fell

"The female is down, I repeat the female is down."

As the team reached the top of the stairs there was an explosion and they retreated into the safety of the stairwell. Commander Chance's screen was filled with smoke. "What the fuck! Do you have eyes on the suspect?"

"Negative. Woman's alive, request Medivac."

"Get your team out of there before the real police turn up. Chance out."

"What do you mean they're not dead?" Annette Chambers could hardly contain her anger.

Adam Chance may have been the commander of a highly trained ATU Special Forces Unit but he was getting his balls roasted by the woman on the other end of the phone.

"All you had to do was blow up a building, kill anyone who got in your way and bring me the bloody laptop! But all you managed to do was to injure Susan Blakeshaw and let Jim Brannigan escape and he still has the fucking laptop!"

She was practically screaming at the top of her voice "Get back here and clear out your office, your days in charge of Jack Shit are over!" And with that, she hung up on Ex-Commander Adam Chance.

She picked up her NMR Phone and called Matt Jones.

"Where are you?... I didn't know he was going to blow up the entire building... I wanted them alive too... He must have had help... Of course, I'm telling you the truth. He had help getting off that roof. Call all the agencies and see what footage you can get and report back to me in one hour."

Matt Jones wasn't so sure, what he'd seen was an assassination attempt, not a seize and recovery operation.

He was a witness to something that made him nervous. He made a few calls to see if anyone had eyes on the roof of Aquarius House just after the explosion. It wasn't long before he got a call back from a friend at MI5. They had picked up chatter from a Russian news helicopter that was covering the explosion. Turns out they left in a hurry only to return a few minutes later, seems like they may have picked up a passenger.

"The Russians have him, looks as though they plucked him off the roof just before Commander-Big-Balls could snatch him. The helicopter didn't log a route but the nearest helipad to St George's is in Battersea. I checked, and they had an unscheduled stop there today, a Russian TV Crew. They only stayed a few minutes. Two men got off but only one got back on. The other left with a young woman. They got into a car with diplomatic plates."

"Shit!" said Annette Chambers.

"What do you want me to do?" asked Matt Jones.

"Nothing, go home, I'll call you later."

Things were unravelling now for Annette Chamber, she had played her hand, and for her to stay alive she needed Brannigan and Bradshaw dead and the laptop secured. As neither had happened yet she had no doubt her life was in danger. She sat in her office wondering where on Earth Jim Brannigan was when her mobile rang.

Only one person had that number, her father, Professor Mike Chambers. She couldn't let him think she was dead after she shot the Right Honourable Carol James. After all, she was the only family he had.

She had contacted him through one of his students in Oxford. The girl, Jenny, was the daughter of a friend of hers; an American diplomat who owed her a favour. Jenny had been asked by her father to play a trick on his old friend Professor Chambers. All she had to do was give her professor a piece of paper with a telephone number on it and say it was from an old friend of his whom she had met the night before. The friend wanted to discuss a personal matter with the professor and he was to call the number from a public phone box at 3 pm the following day and all would be revealed. He was to use the phone box outside Hair Candy on Oxford Street and he mustn't tell anyone or it would ruin the surprise. The friend didn't give his name but said that Professor Chambers would understand once he made the call.

"Dad, what's wrong? You know you should only use this number in an emergency."

"Well, if it isn't Ms. Chambers, recently deceased. I must say you sound in excellent health for a dead woman."

"You bastard! If you hurt him I'll kill you!" she screamed.

"There's no need for anyone to get hurt. You have something I want and I have something you want and I'm not talking about your father. I have no interest in hurting him unless I have to." Brannigan said calmly.

He had located the Professor easily enough through the newspaper article when Mike Chambers had spoken out about his daughter's death. He guessed it must have come as something of a shock to the old man to learn she was alive and well. And there was only one Professor Chambers working at Oxford University after all.

"I'll meet you at the Coffee Dock at Vauxhall Tube Station tomorrow at 8 am with Ms. Blakeshaw. I'm sure you know it; it's where you killed your old boss. Oh, and come alone."

He hung up. He wanted Annette Chambers rattled, if she thought he might hurt her father that could give him an edge. He didn't have much time but he did have the makings of a plan. He left Mike Chambers alive and well but he couldn't help wondering how long he would stay that way.

On the street corner, he passed a newspaper stand stopping briefly when he saw a picture of Alisa Petrov. He picked up the newspaper.

*The young Russian Translator was the victim of a robbery while in Edinburgh visiting friends. She was leaving a nightclub when two youths attempted to snatch her handbag. Alisa fought back when one of the youths pulled a knife and fatally stabbed Ms. Petrov. Edinburgh Police are appealing for witnesses.*

The newspaper vendor wasn't best pleased however, "Hey Mister, this isn't a library. Put the paper down or pay for it."

Brannigan put the paper back on the stand and walked off.

"Fucking tourist," mumbled the vendor.

As he walked to the Apollo Brannigan wondered if the driver killed her when he discovered she had not secured the satellite codes. There was no mention of Alex, Charlie, or Noel, although he guessed their bodies would turn up eventually as three more unconnected tragic incidents somewhere across the UK. Or maybe not: after all, one person goes missing every two minutes in the UK, that's 275,000 Britons that just disappear every year. On second thoughts he wasn't holding out much hope that Alex, Charlie or Noel would be found anytime soon.

## Chapter Fourteen

Shane McGowan sat behind the glass panel "Oh Joy, look who's back."

"Just can't seem to keep away. Can I use your fax machine?"

"How do you know we have a fax machine?" "I'm guessing email hasn't reached here yet, a bit like the hot water."

"It's for the exclusive use of residents, I'm afraid," said Shane a little too smugly.

"Then book me in Shane, one night only."

"My name's not Shane," muttered Shane as he buzzed the door to allow Brannigan into the back office.

At any one time, there are about eighty small, independent newspapers operating in London. They are the ones that are so small that nobody bothers tracking their stories, phone calls or emails and besides faxes were old school and couldn't be easily traced.

These little news outlets were a key part of Brannigan's plan. He wrote his fax, put it in the machine, and hit send to a dozen of London's brightest and best:

*Annette Chambers, responsible for killing the Right Honourable Carol James MP and who was subsequently shot dead by the Metropolitan Police will be at the Coffee Dock in Vauxhall Tube Station at 8.15 am tomorrow.*

"Matt, I need your help with something, strictly off the books." Annette Chambers was reaching out to an old friend. "Just you and me, no one else."

"Okay," replied Matt Jones cautiously.

"I'm listening, what's this all about?"

"Brannigan has my Dad and he says he'll trade his safety and Carter's laptop for Susan Blakeshaw. He wants to do the trade at Vauxhall Tube Station tomorrow morning, 8 am. We're to meet him at the Coffee Dock. You got to admire his stones if nothing else, right under our own house for Christ's sake. You in?" But she got no answer from Special Agent Jones

"We're keeping Blakeshaw in St Aidan's Hospital in Old Camden Town overnight. I can arrange for a car to collect her first thing in the morning, what do you think?"

There was a long silence on the other end of the phone as Matt Jones considered his options.

"Come on Matt, I need your help on this one, it's my Dad we're talking about here."

"I'll collect her," he said at last "Now tell me how are we going to do this thing?"

"We get Susan Blakeshaw from St Aidan's Hospital to the Coffee Dock and then kill them both once we get the Carter file and the laptop. He's a wanted terrorist and she's his accomplice. No one will look too closely at this."

"And who's going to do the killing?" asked Matt Jones. He had no problem killing Jim Brannigan if he had to, but he wanted to see how far Annette Chambers was willing to go. Without hesitation, she replied "I'll do it, I'll hide that little Compact of mine at the Coffee Dock and use it to kill them both. You run interference for me in case any have-a-go hero wants to get in my way" She knew that tomorrow would be her last chance to sort out this mess. She made the call to St Aidan's to arrange the pickup and the trap was set.

Jim Brannigan spent his second night in the Apollo Guest House and he hoped it would be his last. Nothing had changed since he was last there, not even the bed sheets he suspected, so he lay on top of the bed and he thought about tomorrow and Susan. His plan was simple enough, cause a distraction for Chambers with the media and snatch Susan. He knew there would be a trap but he had no time to cover all the angles. He just had to hope he got lucky.

Then he slept. He had taught his body to sleep over the years even in the most stressful situations; in war zones around the world and all his years with ATU. A tired soldier could easily be a dead soldier and besides, tomorrow would bring an end to all of this, one way or the other. He was sure of that.

### Day Six: The Net Closes

Matt Jones arrived at St Aidan's Hospital at 5 am. Susan Blakeshaw was already waiting in reception. Her left shoulder was bandaged, and her left arm was in a sling.

"Who gave the order to shoot me Special Agent Jones?" Her tone was stern, her features set. There was no room for a lie.

"Annette Chambers, Ma'am" came the honest reply.

"And does she know you work for me?"
"No Ma'am"
"Who do we have with us this morning?"
"Agents Fieldhouse and Woods."
"Are they known to Annette Chambers?"
"No Ma'am, that's why I chose them,"
"And what does Ms. Chambers have in store for me this morning? Use me as bait obviously but afterward, what then?"

"You and Brannigan are to die once she has the laptop and the file"

"And what are we going to do about that?"

Susan Blakeshaw, Head of Cyber Terrorism at ATU, sat in the back of the black SUV as it made its way through the early morning traffic into London and onward to Vauxhall Tube Station. Agents Fieldhouse and Woods followed behind in a black SUV of their own. As she gazed out upon the early morning traffic she was lost in her thoughts. She often wondered why she had kept on being Brannigan's analyst long after she had gotten her promotions over the years. He was her last connection to Jennifer of course and she never really blamed him for her death. He could have been more attentive, he let the job get in the way but Michael was the cuckoo in their nest.

She wasn't sorry he was dead but Brannigan wouldn't see it that way. He wouldn't forgive her if he ever found out that she had worked with Sir Alistair McIntyre to create this plan. That as Carter's boss she gave the orders that ultimately led to his death but she had not agreed to the release of Brannigan's photo to the news outlets or the branding of him as a terrorist.

She, perhaps naively, wanted to use him to recover Carter's laptop. She was surprised when McIntyre had her arrested at home on the orders of the Foreign Secretary and agreeing to meet Brannigan in the hospital in an attempt to recover the file was her way of trying to save his life. But he wouldn't understand that either and that vexed her.

Another thing that vexed her was that she underestimated Annette Chambers' ambition. Since she was shot on the roof it was obvious to her that she too was a target but to shoot her as a terrorist was astonishing. However, underestimating Annette Chambers' ambition was a mistake she wasn't about to repeat.

At 6 am the day staff arrived at the Coffee Dock as Joanne Brownley was folding her apron and waiting for Jason McEvoy to arrive.

Joanne was in her mid-fifties and a bit too heavy by her own admission and apart from that nice young man she had spoken to for a while nothing much had happened, it had been a quiet night and takings were down. Still, she had a hot bath and a warm bed to look forward to and as soon as Jason arrived she could get off home. She always looked forward to her early morning banter with Jason as they changed over; checking the till and preparing the previous night's takings for lodging on her way home. She enjoyed his non-PC comments, his cheeky grin and his ready smile; in truth, she flirted with Jason McEvoy and enjoyed every minute of it.

But she didn't recognise the two people standing in front of her this morning.

"Good Morning Joanne, we're the day shift. I'm James and this is Donna."
Joanne nodded but looked confused. "Where's Jason, Jason McEvoy? He does the day shift."

"Phoned in sick, so they sent us to cover."

"Well nobody told me...mind you, nobody tells me anything."

"I know, right? The workers are the last to know," smiled Agent Fieldhouse.

"Yea, well, maybe so. Anyway, the till's been done and the float for the day is in there. You want to check it?"

"Nah, that's alright. We trust you!"

"Don't trust me too much! Remember if the till's short it comes out of your wages honey, not mine!"

Joanne Brownley laughed but couldn't help thinking how two people would fit behind the tiny counter. There was hardly enough room for her and while she'd put on a few inches over the years, she wasn't exactly on the big side. Still, she was keen to get off home and was glad in a way that James or Donna didn't seem the kind for idle chit-chat. She hardly noticed the woman with her arm in a sling walk past.

"Well, I'm off you two. Have fun and remember keep the till right or it comes out of your pocket!"

And with that Joanne Brownley melted into the morning crowd.

At 7 am the two agents were busy serving coffee and breakfast to hungry commuters as Annette Chambers strolled along the platform.

"I fucking hate people" said Donna Woods. "Could this day get any worse?"

James Fieldhouse nodded in the direction of Chambers. "I think her day will be worse than ours. Looks like it's time to make that special coffee of yours."

Annette Chambers opened the door to her office and her unscheduled meeting with Susan Blakeshaw.

"Ms. Chambers, please take a seat. You don't mind if I sit on this side of the desk do you?" There was no question in her voice, so Annette Chambers sat. "Thank you for contacting me yesterday"

"Look Ms. Blakeshaw," Annette Chambers interrupted rather nervously. "As I said, I'm sorry you were shot. My orders to Commander Chance were explicit; no one was to get hurt. It was supposed to be a seize-and-recovery, nothing else. Instead, he blew up the building and shot you." Susan raised her hand to silence Annette Chambers.

"No matter. So you think you can persuade Jim Brannigan to come in and give us the laptop and Carter file." Once again, there was no hint of a question. "Well then, what would you have me do?"

Jim Brannigan got off the early morning tube train from Waterloo and walked casually toward the Coffee Dock. Susan Blakeshaw and Annette Chambers were seated at a table to the right of the bar sipping their coffee; there was a third coffee on the table in front of an empty chair.

"Well Mr. Brannigan, here she is as promised. I assume you have the file and the laptop? Hand them over and you both can be on your way."

"Well the laptop was shot by a Russian agent just after the Echelon codes were downloaded onto a flash drive, this flash drive."
"So, hand them over," repeated Annette Chambers. "The file and the flash drive are leaving with me, and so is Susan."

Annette Chambers scanned the early morning crowd for Matt Jones but there was no sign of him. She sipped slowly on her coffee to buy herself a little more time. She would have to take care of this herself and fuck Matt Jones. She'd make sure his life wasn't worth shit when she finished with him. No one fucks with Annette Chambers and gets away with it. She reached under the table to retrieve the Springfield XDM Compact that she had stashed there the day before but that nice young man who spent time talking to Joanne Brownley had already taken it.

"That wasn't the deal JIM."

"No it wasn't, but we both know there was no deal."

"You won't get out of here alive," she hissed.

"Oh, I think we will. You see in about two minutes a dozen of London's finest reporters are going to turn up to witness a miracle; the resurrection of a radical terrorist who was reportedly shot dead by our brave boys in blue after killing the Right Honourable Carol James and Sir Alistair McIntyre only a few short days ago."

Annette Chambers looked at Susan, she was starting to feel quite ill; she was sweating and feeling nauseous.

"You don't look at all well," said Susan, "Not well at all". There was no sympathy in her voice and Brannigan realised there was another plan at play. He didn't know whose, but he knew it wasn't his. Chambers looked at Brannigan, "She....she's the one. Carter, Logan..." Her speech was slurred and she couldn't think clearly anymore.

"That'll be the Demerol in the coffee starting to work. You really shouldn't have told Commander Chance to shoot me," said Susan

On cue at approximately 8.15 am a small but determined group of men and women armed with cameras and voice recorders descended on Annette Chambers. Among them were reporters from the Croydon Guardian, the Barking and Dagenham Post and the Docklands and East London Advertiser. Cameras flashed, and the feeding frenzy began, but Annette Chambers was beyond their questions.

Her heart was racing, and she fell to the ground and went into some kind of seizure. Her time at the big table was over. Susan Blakeshaw had underestimated her for the last time and in those final moments she must have realised that she was dying. Darkness came to her and wrapped its pain and fear around her beating heart and it claimed her for its own.

London Transport Police rushed to the scene and a doctor stepped out of the crowd to administer first aid but there was no saving Annette Chambers. The cameras continued to roll as Susan Blakeshaw and Jim Brannigan slipped away from the platform and Annette Chambers died for a second time.

Susan grabbed Brannigan by the arm, "Give me the file and the flash drive Jim, I have a plan." The look on Brannigan's face told her he wasn't going to give up the files anytime soon.

"What just happened?" he asked.

"I did a deal with Special Agent Jones to save our lives. He told me I was to be exchanged for the laptop and the file and then you and I were to be killed."

"But why would he do that Susan?

"Look, Jim, I've known Matt Jones for a few years, we even dated for a while. He told me Annette Chambers' plan as a courtesy, nothing more. I asked him if he could do anything. He told me I was to leave the laptop and file on Chambers' desk. And that's what I'm going to do."

"How'd you know he would kill Chambers?"

"He said he worked for the Head of Cyber Security and that Chambers had become a liability. She thought he was helping her but he had his orders!"

"And who is the head of Cyber Security?"

"I don't know!" yelled Susan. "He wouldn't tell me! And why are you interrogating me?! Just this once, trust someone, trust me!" Reluctantly Brannigan handed her the file and the flash drive.

"I'll meet you at Gatwick Airport, and from there we can get to Dublin. I know someone who can help us."

Susan nodded and walked down the corridor and took the lift to the third floor. Brannigan headed for the busy streets above and onward to Gatwick .

Susan entered Annette Chamber's office. She placed the Carter File and the flash drive neatly on the desk as arranged. On top of that, she put her security pass and hoped Agent Jones would understand. She closed the door gently and left ATU for the last time. She walked out through the grey door, down the grey steps and continued walking a block or two before hailing a taxi.

Brannigan was waiting for her at the airport, with two tickets to Dublin on EasyJet flight EJ9230. From there they could go anywhere in the world, and be anyone they wanted to be. There were fake passports aplenty in the Emerald Isle if you knew the right people and Jim Brannigan knew the right people.

Gabriella Santini sat nervously at her desk.

"Yes, I have them...Yes, the flash drive and the file...Just where you said they would be... No, he doesn't know I have them and there was something else on the desk, Susan Blakeshaw's ID... Yes, I took that as well. I have them ready for collection. What time will the courier get here? Okay."

Gabriella Santini hung up her very own NMR phone, placed it and a small jiffy bag in the top drawer of her desk and locked the drawer, and continued working on her computer.

A few moments later Matt Jones strode past without even acknowledging her presence and entered Annette Chambers' office. He looked at the desk and around the room. No sign of the flash drive and file. "Shit!" He took out his phone. "Hi Li, it's Matt Jones, I have some information you might find useful...I know we haven't spoken in years, but this is about the murder of the Chinese delegates in Edinburgh....No, it wasn't North Korea. Meet me in ten minutes in Mr. Wang's and I'll tell you all about it."

Li Xiu Ying was an agent of the CIA, the Chinese Intelligence Agency, an agency responsible for counter-intelligence and the promotion of Chinese interests around the world, including boosting trade with non-EU countries such as the soon-to-be Neo-Democratic State of Great Britain.

Along with the UK, China helped make up the United Nations Security Council and since 1946 they have worked regularly together on joint operations to maintain 'international peace and security': at least that's what it says in the brochure. In reality, it's an exchange program for spies and it was through this program that Matt Jones first met Li Xiu Ying. Her name means 'elegant and brave'. Matt Jones often thought it should also include deadly and determined.

It's widely known that the Chinese are systematically buying up huge parts of the world and its infrastructure. They are especially interested in anything that can be used to control or track people, so they invest heavily in power supplies, aviation, hotel chains, transport networks and Information Technology. Matt Jones was sure of it, Li Xiu Ying would be just the girl to help him find a couple of runaways with secrets to hide. It looked like he would get that face-to-face with Jim Brannigan after all.

Mr. Wang's is a small, noisy Asian restaurant in London. It can only seat about 15 people so the serving hatch that faces out onto the street is alive with eager hands stretching for the wondrous little boxes of food heaven. People scurry away, hunched over on nearby benches and steps or perhaps back to their desks to devour their contents.

Despite the demand for space inside there was always a small red table reserved for staff from a nearby Chinese office block that was just around the corner from ATU. Li Xiu Ying was one of about five hundred people who worked there and she was already seated when Matt Jones arrived.

"I don't have much time here Matt. We're looking at our friends in the North for that job you mentioned."

"I'd recommend you take a look at a man by the name of Jim Brannigan. He has done some work for us in the past but is freelance at the moment."

"Yes, part of a terrorist cell apparently but our latest Intel says he's not looking good for the job in Edinburgh."

"Look Li, your Intel's wrong. He's a soldier turned jihad radical and it was his team that killed your delegates in Edinburgh. He's travelling with a woman, Susan Blakeshaw, on fake passports. It will take us too long to find them because we don't have your Single Token Travel Technology yet."

"And what is it you think you know about STT?"

"We know you have it. We know you've been installing it in travel networks across the Globe and that includes the UK travel network, most of which you own. We know it uses a three-way multiple recognition technique to confirm individual identity so accurately that you would never need to use a passport or identity card ever again. My guess is they'll head for Dublin then make a jump into Europe, possibly France."

"What makes you think they'll head for Dublin?"

"Cause it's what I'd do. Don't bullshit me here Li, I need your help on this one. If we don't get them back to ATU Headquarters in the next twenty-four hours they'll be gone and we'll be in the shit."

"There's something you're not telling me here Matt, isn't there?" Li Xiu Ying waited patiently for Matt Jones to make up his mind.

"They have the Echelon Codes too."

"Jesus Matt! When you Brits fuck up, you fuck up big.....does the rest of the U.N. Security Council know about this?"

"I don't think so, well not that I know of any way and I'd like to keep it like that."

"Send me any photos, voice recordings and video files you have on them. I'll come back to you in a couple of hours. If they've been through any UK airport or used any transport network we'll find them, fake passports or not....and you owe me," replied Li Xiu. She knew Matt Jones had been somewhat economical with the truth. China knew the Brexit data had been compromised but losing the Echelon Codes was news. China was already one of the UK's biggest trading partners but it would be in China's interests to increase trade post-Brexit, so she'd play along for a while.

## Chapter Fifteen

Dublin Airport carries upwards of 80,000 passengers a day and, like all airports since 9/11, it has strict security protocols. Even so, at the passport control, Nicola Drake was checked and waved through and just behind her Frank Parks stepped forward.

"What's the purpose of your visit....Mr. Parks?"

"Pleasure, just here with my girlfriend for a few days."

The Police Officer paused for a moment, closed the passport and handed it back to Brannigan."You have a nice time." "Thanks, I will." Just two more people spending a few days in the nation's capital.

After a quick stop at an airport photo booth they made their way to the nearest exit and a taxi ride to Toddy's bar, Gresham Hotel, Connelly Street, Dublin. They settled into a small table in the far corner of the bar away from the draught of the front door and ordered a pint of Guinness and Bloody Mary. "Louis, it's me...I know, it's been too long... I'll meet you in Toddy's in twenty minutes."

"Who was that?" asked Susan quietly so as not to be overheard by Eamon, the friendly barman who when he wasn't serving customers seemed to spend his time polishing the life out the glasses that surrounded him.

"Louis Cartwright"

"And can Louis Cartwright be trusted?"

"No, but for a few hundred euros Louis can get us two genuine Irish passports. These are real passports Susan, sold to criminal gangs by drug addicts, whores, and the homeless. And since Louis runs the biggest criminal gang in North Dublin he has an endless supply of passports."

"Can they be traced?"

"That's the beauty of this system. The passports are not reported lost or stolen so they can be scanned at any airport in the world without triggering any security protocol. The only downside is that you have to be the person on the passport. So the tricky bit is picking someone who looks vaguely like you in the first place. But after all, how many people look exactly like their passport photograph?" said Brannigan smiling.

"And how long will this take?" asked Susan.

"Few hours maybe"

Brannigan was taking a risk because Louis' main concern was Louis and he would do anything to turn a coin, including ratting out an old friend. Still, there were only a few ways of getting your hands on an Irish passport and Louis knew them all. Some were even legal, like buying one under the Irish Government's 'Economic Citizenship Policy' for a few million Euros. Others required a little more creativity, like paying a contact in the passport office a few thousand Euros not to look too closely at a passport application request. But these both took time, time Brannigan didn't have. So, for a few hundred Euros, Louis Cartwright could get you one of the 20,000 Irish passports being sold on the streets of Dublin every day.

    He also had access to a Nigerian forger who could replace the photo on the passport to such a high standard that no one or no device could tell the difference. As an extra service, he could do a criminal and financial background check to ensure there were no outstanding warrants or restrictions on your new identity. The deluxe service included a bank account and cards in your new name, although that could take as long as a week to arrange. No wonder then that Ireland was the 'gateway to Europe' for everything from money laundering to people smuggling and maybe the odd act of terrorism.

    Twenty minutes or so later a rather ordinary-looking man of medium height and medium build with no distinguishing marks of any kind approached their table. In fact the only remarkable thing about this man was that no one could ever really remember seeing him. If this man was any more unmemorable he might just be a ghost and that's the way Louis Cartwright liked it.

He smiled his ready smile and extended a hand to Brannigan. There was nothing average about the handshake. Any doubts that Louis meant business faded as cyanosis quickly set into the fingertips of the poor unfortunate on the receiving end of that welcome. Brannigan held both the handshake and the eye contact firm until Louis released first and sat down. He didn't look at or acknowledge Susan in any way.

"What are you looking for?"

"Two passports, in two hours." It wasn't a request and it wasn't taken as such, Louis Cartwright had worked with Brannigan before and knew that too many questions could be detrimental to his health, in a permanent sort of way.

"Back here in two hours then?" said Louis.

"No, we'll need to move on. McIvor's on Palace Street, and don't stiff me on the price." He handed Louis the photographs from the photo booth, "Just in case you can't get a good match" and he watched as this far-from-average man disappeared onto Connolly Street.

"You said he can't be trusted, is it wise to use him?" asked Susan quietly.

"No, but he's a businessman and as long as it's in his business interests to work with me we'll be fine, at least until we pay him."

"And is it really that easy to get Irish passports here?"

"Yea, I told you, everyone uses them; Israeli secret service, Russian spies, everyone. It's the worst kept secret in the secret service world and that's a problem for the UK after Brexit. That's why some see a hard border in Northern Ireland as essential to the security of the United Kingdom."

This was all mildly interesting but not at all what Brannigan wanted to talk to Susan about. He changed the subject somewhat abruptly.

"What happened back there, Susan? I realise we couldn't discuss it on the plane, but I need to know"

"I did a deal with agent Jones to save our lives" Susan replied quietly. The lack of a response compelled her to continue "We've already gone over this!"

"Tell me again," said Brannigan.

"He told me I was to be exchanged for the laptop and the Carter file and then you and I were to be killed." She could almost feel the heat coming from Brannigan's stare. "He told me Annette Chambers' plan and I asked him if he could do anything. He said he could if I left the laptop and file on Chambers' desk. I asked him when and all he said was I'd know. So, when Chambers died that's what I did. I also left my ID badge because I think it's time we both disappeared. End of story."

There was awkwardness between them now and a curtain of silence fell for a time. Eventually, Susan spoke. "And where do you suggest I go while you meet Mr. Congeniality?"

Brannigan looked over her shoulder at the hotel stand advertising tourist sites and tours around Dublin. There was one for a tour of the Guinness Storehouse Factory. "I know the very place."

Palace Street is officially Dublin's smallest street with only two addresses; No1 Palace Street which is now Mc Ivor's and No2 Palace Street which was, until recently, owned by The Sick and Indigent Room Keeper's Society (1855 to 1992) and now boasted 'bird's nest' accommodation for the thirty-somethings that frequented the likes of McIvor's next door.

Mc Ivor's itself was once a Dockers' pub, providing succour and solitude for the men who worked the Dublin Docks. Men who worked hard and drank harder, but the docks had long gone. In the 1970s Dublin's docks suffered the same fate as docklands across the Globe and Cruise Liners now replaced coal ships and the warehouses were now fine apartments, boutique hotels, and bistros. McIvor's was now a 'wine and cocktail' bar where bright young things in suits and dresses gathered after work and ordered Pinot Grigio and Sex-on-the-Beach.

The laughter of success filled the air when Brannigan pushed open one of two original warehouse doors and sauntered over to Louis Cartwright sitting at the bar.

"Five hundred.... each," said Louis. He slid an envelope across the bar.

"I asked you not to stiff me on the price"
"Listen, you're hot property, my friend. You and that little woman of yours, you're lucky I'm even talking to you."

Brannigan thought it curious that Louis should talk to him like that, disrespectful in a way. He knew Louis was not to be messed with but equally Louis knew all about Jim Brannigan and what he was capable of. It seemed curious that Louis would goad him like that unless he had sold him out. "Don't ever make the mistake of thinking we're friends."

"Look, no offence. Word is that the Chinese are after you, something about an explosion in Scotland a few days ago. They know you're here by the way. My Nigerian friend has been threatened and bribed in equal measure to report any activity involving anyone who might even look like either of you two."

"Can you trust him?"

"No, but I pay him well and he knows I can protect him if it comes to that, at least in North Dublin anyway. The Chinese are everywhere now man; they own half the country, including the airlines and the power grids, and what they don't own they control through their gangs. It's getting so a decent criminal can hardly make a living anymore."

Brannigan almost laughed out loud, "I never thought of you as decent."

He put one thousand euros down on the bar and left, sweeping the passports up as he went. No one took any notice as music blared above the noise of the TV screens that adorned every wall showing sports from around the world that nobody watched. The old warehouse door swung slowly closed behind him and Palace Street was silent once more.

## Chapter Sixteen

It didn't take long for Li to have a trace on Brannigan and Blakeshaw. She had followed Matt Jones's hunch and found out that Frank Parks and Nicola Drake were in Dublin. Transport and security cameras traced their movements over the last few hours from Dublin Airport. Susan Blakeshaw was on a tour of the Guinness factory and Jim Brannigan was in McIvor's wine and cocktail bar in Dublin Docks with a known criminal, one Louis Cartwright. It would be easier to take them separately, more discrete with less likelihood of having to kill them. Chinese agents would lift them both as they were already in position and had sight of the targets.

On the smallest street in Dublin three Chinese agents moved quickly forward with intent. The man and woman to Brannigan's right seemed focused, calm almost, clearly intent on doing him harm at the earliest possible opportunity. The man running hard on his left however was in full flight mode, adrenalin rushing through his body. His right arm was drawn backward, the knife in his right hand already visible, ready to rip and tear into flesh and bone. Seconds passed and Brannigan readied himself for the onslaught and relaxed his body.

The knife-wielding maniac with the crazy eyes would hit first. Brannigan knew better than to get fixated on the weapon. The blade might be the deadliest part of the attack, but any movement of the arm starts in the upper torso. Brannigan knew three things; he had to hit hard, he had to hit first and he was going to get cut. He was hoping that this nut job wouldn't appreciate that this wasn't his first knife fight and besides, Jim Brannigan wasn't dead until the Coroner said so.

The first attacker lunged forward and Brannigan stepped into the assault, interrupting the momentum of the strike. His left arm came up to block the attack while his right fist hit hard into the attacker's right shoulder knocking him backward. The agent slashed the knife instinctively toward Brannigan. Brannigan twisted away from the flashing blade and pulled his head back as far as he could, but the knife cut deep into his left shoulder as his left knee crushed the man's genitals and the attacker with the crazy eyes collapsed to the ground.

The other two attackers must have smelled blood because they flung themselves at Brannigan in a frenzied attack. The woman struck first, leaping off her feet, coming down on top of Brannigan, delivering a crushing blow to the side of his head. Brannigan reeled backward just as the man followed through with an almighty kick to the chest. Jim Brannigan was down…but not out.

He jumped up onto one knee and as the woman charged forward once more he sprang forward and upwards delivering a mighty uppercut to the underside of her jaw. Her head cracked backward, and she lifted off her feet for the second time. The man meanwhile rained punches into Brannigan. Brannigan tried to block them with his left arm but the pain from the knife wound was searing through his body. He shoved forward into his attacker, pushing him hard against the cold brick wall of number 2 Palace Street, and in a last desperate effort his right fist pounded furious punches into the assailant's torso, rib cage and face. Eventually, the man crumpled to the ground. Breathless, exhausted, and bleeding after thirty violent seconds Jim Brannigan was the last man standing.

His shoulder was throbbing, the pain was excruciating. All he could do was focus on staying conscious. His phone rang; no caller ID. Since he only had this phone all of two hours he was intrigued; he answered but didn't speak. To be fair he didn't think he could speak.

It was a Chinese voice, a female Chinese voice, "Mr. Brannigan please look to your left and up to the big screen above the Santander Bank."

He did as he was told and saw a huge neon image of Susan in between two smiling Chinese suits, arms wrapped tightly around her outside the Guinness Storehouse. Across the bottom of the screen, there was a banner that read: 'To Jim, all my love. Hope to see you again soon.'

The voice on the other end of the phone spoke once more "Now Mr. Brannigan you will return to ATU Headquarters in London within the next twenty-four hours. Failure to do so will result in Ms. Blakeshaw's demise. You will not be followed because we don't need to follow you. Please nod if you understand."

Brannigan nodded and a huge grinning emoji appeared on the big screen in front of him before exploding into a rainbow of colour. The phone went dead; he guessed the conversation was over.

"Well, I think we need to order a Chinese Takeaway here. Oh, and get you to a doctor before you pass out." Louis Cartwright stood behind Brannigan and smiled his ready smile, chuckling at his own absurd joke. "It'll cost you of course, but I reckon you're good for it."

Brannigan reckoned Louis Cartwright was waiting in McIvor's to see how things would work out in the street before he offered any kind of help to his old friend. That was something Jim Brannigan wouldn't forget or forgive in a hurry.

A few hours later he was sitting up in a hospital bed, his wound was stitched, the anti-nausea drug was working wonderfully and the lidocaine injected into his shoulder ensured he was pain-free. An IV drip hung from a bed stand feeding fluids and morphine into his bloodstream. He was all set for a good night's sleep. The problem was it was already after midnight and he had a flight to catch. He removed the drip, got dressed and left. Two of Louis' men on his room door made no effort to stop him. He got some oxycodone from the nurse and made his way to Dublin Airport.

Susan Blakeshaw sat uncomfortably at a table in a small room underneath Vauxhall Tube Station as trains rumbled on the tracks above. Matt Jones entered and sat opposite her. "You mind telling me what the hell is going on here SUSAN?"

"I don't know what you mean Special Agent Jones, and don't you still work for me?"

"Nice try SUSAN, but you stopped working for ATU when you double-crossed me and stole the Carter file and the satellite codes."

"I left them as agreed."

"Well then, where the FUCK are they?"

"No, the question is who took them and why?"

"Nah, you're bluffing. You kept them and ran away to Dublin with Jim Brannigan. Tell me where they are or you go to jail for the rest of your life!"

"Don't be absurd! I went to Dublin to get clear of this mess and to get Jim Brannigan off our backs. Check the security footage; you'll see me enter the building at around 8.30 this morning. I left again around 5 minutes later, as agreed."

"So, where are the files?"

"Stolen, I assume. Why don't you check the log to see who swiped into Chambers' Office between 8.30 and 9.00 am? Apart from me and you, of course."

Matt Jones made a call. "This is Special Agent Jones. Give me the swipe card information for room 23 between 8.30 and 9.00 this morning...Three entries...You sure...Okay, thanks." He put his phone down and turned to Susan. "Looks like Annette Chambers let herself in at 8.47 am. Approximately 30 minutes after she died."

"Okay, so we know the when. Now for the who, whoever has them will want to get them out of the building discretely."

"So we lock the building down and search everyone."

"We could, but we may never find them. Besides, they'd want the files out of the building as soon as possible. Check with the front desk to see if there have been any unscheduled deliveries or collections today."

Matt Jones used his phone once more, putting it on speaker. "Hi Bob, it's Matt Jones here. I need you to check something for me."

"Sure thing Matt, what is it?" "Have there been any last-minute requests for deliveries or collections today?"

"Let me check the log...Yea, a package was delivered today at 1.13 pm....let me see...request sheet says it was power of attorney papers for a terminally ill father...signature required....signed for by Gabriella Santini."

"Thanks Bob." He hung up the phone and looked at Susan.

"Gabriella's father died two years ago in Italy," she said.

Gabriella Santini now sat in the same seat that Susan had sat in just a few moments earlier. Matt Jones and Sharon Millar sat opposite her. Agent Millar began the interrogation, "We're searching your apartment as we speak, and we will find the file and the codes. What happens to you is up to you."

"Listen, I'm not putting myself in harm's way here. I'll tell you what you want to know." said Gabriella Santini.

"Who do you work for?" asked Special Agent Jones.

"I'm MI5, and have been since they signed me up at a recruitment fair in my last year at University. Joining ATU was my first and only assignment."

"And what is it you do here?" asked Special Agent Jones.

"My brief was simple, do the job I was hired to do at ATU and feed everything back to the MI5 recording centre at Thames House."

"You don't expect us to believe this bullshit, do you? MI5 agents spying on other agencies!" shouted Matt Jones.
"I'm not an agent. I have an apartment in Kensington and a boyfriend who works for Barclays Bank for Christ's sake. I'm not some sort of spy!"

"Are there any more MI5 agents working at ATU then?!" It was Agent Millar's turn to shout.

"I've already told you, I'm not an agent and I wouldn't know anything about that but possibly. I really do work for ATU and I'm good at my job. All I know is that I am one of hundreds of MI5 staff working across all the government departments in the UK, legitimately and permanently. All we do is send back information that is analysed. Anything useful is extracted and may be used somewhere down the line. That's all I know."

"So why take the Carter file and risk being caught?" asked Matt Millar.

"I got an encrypted email this morning telling me to lift the file and flash drive and ensure they were delivered to Thomas House for safekeeping. There wasn't much time, so I used the excuse of needing to sign the power of attorney papers for my poor late father on the request form so that I could get a courier into the building. I didn't think anyone would check. As I said, I'm not a field agent."

"Thomas House?" asked Sharon Millar

"Yes, Thomas House. It's one of several secure storage facilities across London used by MI5 since World War Two. Above ground it offers office space to rent by the hour. The Basement is a different matter. Very Hi-tec security by all accounts!"

"How do you send back this information?"

"Automatically, through a camera in my contact lenses."

"And you'd be wearing these contact lenses now?"

"Yes."

"Leave your ID at reception on the way out." replied Matt Jones.

## Day Seven: The Last Day
## Chapter Seventeen

Once again Jim Brannigan found himself standing on the steps of a grey building in Vauxhall Cross. The front door opened, and he was escorted to the third floor and into Cube One; the irony was not lost on him.

Now Matt Jones sat behind the desk, agents Fieldhouse and Woods sat on the sofa and Brannigan stood. There was no offer of a seat this time. Jones would not be taken so easily again should the need arise. Brannigan recognised Fieldhouse and Woods from the Coffee Dock and now had a fair idea of how Annette Chambers died. He didn't know them or their particular skill sets. He realised he could actually be in trouble this time.

"I had hoped the Chinese would have killed you," said a rather exasperated Matt Jones.

"They did their best, it just wasn't good enough. Then again, neither was yours." The air inside the cube bristled with animosity.

"I could kill you now."

"You could try.....how's the nose by the way?" Matt Jones ignored the jibe.

"Seems like you still have friends here at ATU. You've managed somehow to get out of this mess with your life and I'm sorry to say that my orders are to release you. The codes and file are gone, practically everyone connected to this case is dead and we've uncovered a mole within ATU. As I said, you're free to go."

Jim Brannigan laughed out loud and shook his head. "You still haven't worked this thing out yet, have you? This has all been about National Security and that means MI5. The Government triggered a Brexit vote as a means to create something called a Neo-Democratic State. Sir Alistair McIntyre told me as much in this very room a few days ago. But MI5 have always had their own agenda, they don't answer to anyone but their Director General, and they have never trusted the USA.

I'd say they believe that the Americans will conspire to create fake trade deals with this new state that will collapse Britain's economy and allow the Chinese to buy up even more UK assets. MI5 want to force another referendum vote, that's probably why they leaked the file to John Carter in the first place. Maybe they thought he'd leak the information onto the web. Instead, he got quite a few people killed."

"You have no evidence for any of this," replied Matt Jones.

"It's the only thing that makes sense" continued Brannigan. "Besides when that didn't work they switched to plan B and have been undermining the PM's position in public ever since to try and force another vote. The government's head of MI5, the Home Secretary, resigned along with the Foreign Secretary; all of this piles pressure on the PM and makes another vote more likely. Whoever has the Carter file wins. And don't even get me started on the satellite codes"

"Even if what you say is true, there's nothing you can do about it. Just go and consider yourself lucky!"

"Our definitions of luck may differ slightly Special Agent Jones. Besides I'm not leaving here without Susan Blakeshaw."

Susan Blakeshaw was listening to the conversation in Cube One through an earwig in Matt Jones' ear.

"Tell him I've already been released and he is to meet me outside the Young Vic Theatre in twenty minutes," said Susan.

"She's already been released, said something about meeting some old soldier outside the Young Vic in 20 minutes."

"How do I know you're telling me the truth?"

"You don't, now get out before I shoot you. You're still a wanted terrorist."

Brannigan turned to leave and didn't look back at Matt Jones. "We'll meet again Jonesy, I'm sure of it only it won't be as pleasant for you next time. I promise." It was a childish thing to say of course but he couldn't help himself. Besides he had a feeling it was true. He was escorted to the front door and made his way to the Young Vic.

There was no sign of Susan when he got there. He hung around just inside the foyer of the building so as not to attract any unwanted attention. Besides, he didn't know if Special Agent Jones was joking about the whole terrorist thing so he decided not to take any chances.

He saw her coming through the early afternoon crowd and stepped out to greet her. She reminded him so much of Jennifer. In all that they had been through these last few days, he had grown to care for her, love her even.

Susan saw him standing in the doorway of the theatre; tall and handsome, casually dressed, with his hands resting by his side. She rushed to embrace him, and they kissed like it was the most natural thing in the world, two people in love, together and happy.... until the shot rang out.

## Chapter Eighteen

"What do you mean you're in charge? Who the fuck put you in charge?" shouted Ex-Commander Chance.

"I'm the Senior Field Agent and you'll do as you're damn well told!" shouted Agent Jones, "I want her protected at all times, do you understand? You dumb fuck!" Chance and Jones were standing toe-to-toe in the stairwell,

Chance the taller of the two by a few inches while Jones looked the fitter, with the physique of a boxer or a fighter of some sort. The only real question seemed to be who was going to throw the first punch. The door leading to the third floor swung open.

"Boys, boys, boys, you really should have learned to leave these antics in the playground." The voice was self-assured and ever so slightly mocking, "If you two are ever going to work together you'd better get over yourselves."

Amelia Gallagher stood in the stairwell between floors three and four and gave them both a slightly withering look of disapproval.

"Who *are* you?" They said almost in unison.

"I'm your new boss," said Amelia Gallagher. "Appointed by the Home Secretary about…" she looked at her watch for dramatic effect, "three minutes ago and I find my two most senior staff squabbling on the stairs like a couple of school kids. Let me be clear gentlemen I want you to step up or step out. Follow me."

She turned on her heel and left. Jones and Chance looked at each other in disbelief. Matt Jones shrugged his shoulders.

Amelia Gallagher knew nothing about anti-terrorism, fake news, or the work of ATU but what she did know about was people. She knew how to get the best out of them, how to make them believe that they wanted what she wanted. In short, she knew how to manipulate them.

Chance and Jones followed her into the Director's Office.

"Now, what was all that shouting about?" she asked in a vaguely disinterested way; the way a teacher might ask two unruly children.

"He started it!" exclaimed Ex-Commander Chance, briefly glancing over to Special Agent Jones before staring at the floor.

Amelia Gallagher sighed, "I know all about recent events," she said quietly.

"Then you'll know that Susan Blakeshaw agreed to persuade Jim Brannigan to retrieve the Carter File from MI5 in return for their freedom. Without the file, MI5 has no leverage over the PM for a second vote on Brexit and we can spin the Government out of trouble and back on track".

Matt Jones spoke confidently and with authority and continued. "MI5 have been one step ahead of us all along. We got rid of one mole but that doesn't mean there are no others. We must assume they know what we've agreed with Blakeshaw so an assassination attempt would not be unexpected. I was just persuading commander big-balls here to employ standard countermeasures for such a possibility until we have the file."

"Why not just move the file or copy it?" asked Amelia Gallagher. It was Matt Jones's turn to sigh. "Because if they move it they know we'll know where to in a few hours, so what's the point of that? And they won't want to copy it because then they'll have two files to protect instead of one. Who are you again by the way?"

"My name is Amelia Gallagher and I'm the new, new, temporary Director of ATU, which means as I said, I'm your boss" She looked from Chance to Jones and back again. "Are we clear?" "Yes, Ma'am" came the somewhat reluctant replies.

"Right then Adam, you head over to the Young Vic and make sure you have eyes on the assets; kill anyone who approaches with intent. If you're not sure about the intent kill them anyway, we need that file back. Matt, I need a list of MI5 staff working within ATU". Agent Jones must have looked a bit perplexed. "Fill in an AS120 request form and submit it to queries@MI5.co.uk. Since 9/11 all security agencies must share personnel data to reduce risk to life or property within the UK; see if any faces show up."

"What about the satellite codes?" asked Matt Jones.

"Changed as soon as MI5 acquired the flash drive," replied Amelia Gallagher. "Oh, and get me, Millar and Roberts."

It had been quite a day for Alisha Porter. That morning she had been processing expense claims for field staff when she got a call to report to the Director's Office. Gabriella Santini had gotten some big promotion and they needed someone with office experience to help the new Director for a few days and now Agent Jones and Commander Chance were standing in front of her desk discussing tactics!

"I'll get two four-man teams in position on Bayliss Road, one clean up in an ambulance and one snatch squad in an unmarked van, just in case," said Chance.

"Okay, I'll meet you on Bayliss Road," replied Matt Jones. He turned to leave.

"Commander Big Balls!, is that the best

you could come up with?" laughed Adam Chance.

"It's all I had." smiled Matt Jones. "But remember, I'm in charge of this one...Big Balls." They both smiled.

Alisha Porter pressed the intercom on her desk. "Agents Millar and Roberts to see you, Ma'am."

"Send them in" replied Amelia Gallagher. Ms. Porter pressed another button on her desk and the Director's door clicked open.

"Right, Sharon and Jason, you two get over to the Young Vic theatre in Waterloo, surveillance only on Brannigan and Blakeshaw, no contact. Anything suspicious, radio through to Special Agent Jones; he's taking point on this one. Any questions?" She didn't wait for a reply "Good, get going" She didn't mention Commander Chance and his team, this operation was on a need-to-know basis.

Commander Adam Chance figured that since he was on his way to Waterloo under orders from the new, new, temporary Director of ATU he was reinstated and to hell with the late Annette Chambers. He collected his HK417 rifle from the armoury on the ground floor of Vauxhall Cross and arranged with his squad to have two 4-man teams on standby as agreed with Special Agent Jones.

The tallest building with a direct line of sight on The Young Vic is Croydon House, an office block with no security and easy access to the roof. It was a few streets from the theatre and from this vantage point Commander Chance could see that his teams were in place and that Jim Brannigan was pacing anxiously outside the theatre entrance. As he watched Brannigan he realised they maybe weren't so different; ex-military, no good at anything but taking orders and killing people. Both had no family, no one to care for, and no one to care for them. Commander Chance thought that maybe he was going soft because he was even starting to like that prick Matt Jones.

Jason Roberts and Sharon Millar hadn't worked together long. He was interested in motorbikes and surfing and weekends away with his girlfriend. He didn't know what Sharon Millar was interested in. He realised he knew almost nothing about her. She was nice enough and didn't say too much. That suited him fine. Jason Roberts loved to talk, mostly about himself. Still, he trusted Millar and knew she always had his back, and in this job that's all that mattered.

He grabbed the car keys from the security box just ahead of Sharon Millar and sauntered towards a black SUV. "You snooze, you lose Millar!"

"I only snooze when I'm with you, Roberts," laughed Sharon Millar.

"And why is that Millar?"

"Cause all you talk about is yourself." She mimicked Roberts. "My motorbike, my girlfriend, my next big adventure, blah, blah, blah."

They climbed into the SUV and it roared out into the London Traffic. As they crossed London Roberts talked and Millar listened or at least listened as much as she ever did. "You realise Millar that I know almost nothing about you? You never talk about yourself, like your private self, whereas you know all about me!"

"You do over-disclose, Roberts."

"Nah! We're partners; we're supposed to know things about each other. But I trust you 'cause I know you have my back and that's all that matters, right?" He glanced over to Sharon Millar. "Right?"

"Whatever you say, Roberts, whatever you say."

They parked their black SUV on Waterloo Road, and from there they had a clear view of the theatre entrance, the streets on either side of it, and Waterloo Green beyond. "Wonder how long we'll have to wait? I've plans for tonight," said Roberts.

"Not long," replied Millar. She nodded towards the train station. Susan Blakeshaw could be seen mingling with the early afternoon crowd. Jason Roberts lifted his radio.

"We've eyes on Blakeshaw."

His head smacked against the side window of the SUV as Sharon Millar's fist smashed into his left temple, knocking him unconscious.

"Guess you'll have to cancel those plans, Roberts."

She unclipped her M9 Beretta from its shoulder strap and got out of the vehicle. An M9 Berretta isn't standard issue for an MI5 agent but it was the favoured weapon of Mossad, the Israeli Secret Service and, as a 'leave behind', it might just create a little confusion for GCHQ and embarrassment for the government if the favoured weapon of one of their closest allies and business partners was found at a murder scene. She left Agent Roberts to his dreams and fell in step behind Blakeshaw. Killing her wouldn't be a problem, not getting killed by Jim Brannigan would be a huge problem if he spotted her. She dropped back into the crowd leaving the station.

Matt Jones' laptop pinged with an email from MI5 labelled *AS120 request*. He opened the file and read through the list of names, one stood out: Sharon Millar. "Christ!" He grabbed his radio off the desk.

"Commander Chance, do you copy?! Sharon Millar is an MI5 agent. I say again, Sharon Millar is an MI5 agent. She is to be considered armed and dangerous. We are currently unable to contact her or Agent Roberts. Do you copy?"

"No shit Sherlock!" was the reply from Commander Chance.

Susan Blakeshaw was unaware of the Agent following her and practically ran toward the theatre and into the outstretched arms of Jim Brannigan. As they embraced Sharon Millar drew her gun, took up the tactical shooting stance so familiar to law enforcement and in that moment, she died. A bullet from an HK417 sniper rifle ripped into the left side of her head, the momentum of the gunshot threw her sideward to the ground and removed the right side of her face.

Jim Brannigan pulled Susan towards himself and backward into the foyer of the theatre, where they stumbled and fell. The stable doors swung closed but failed to drown out the screaming and panic. Armed Response would be there in minutes, so they had to move and move fast. "Follow me, and keep up."

Brannigan lifted Susan to her feet and they bolted through the front of house, through the auditorium, through the backstage area, and down a narrow corridor to the stage door that exited onto Webber Road.

"Alpha Team move in. Captain Gerard, I want surveillance on Brannigan and Blakeshaw, currently exiting the stage door of the Young Vic Theatre onto Webber Road. Do not intercept, I'll relocate and keep in touch. Oh, and get one of our hygiene teams to clean the road, we don't want the Mayor up in arms about a little blood on the sidewalk, not when he's got all those stabbings to deal with, Chance out." He placed the rifle in the grip bag at his feet and headed for the stairs.

They walked purposefully through the mid-morning crowds and away from the sirens and the dead woman with half a face. When Brannigan thought they'd walked far enough they ducked into a McDonald's and sat over a couple of black coffees.

"What just happened?" asked Susan, sobbing.
Brannigan reached out and held her hand across the table.

"We're in trouble here Susan, Agent Millar was killed because she came after us, I've no idea why she came after us and I don't know who killed her, so I don't know who we can trust. I do know we can't survive on our own."

"Listen Jim" Susan began. "When I was being held at ATU Matt Jones told me that the Carter File was taken by MI5 to Thomas House over in Pimlico for storage. I think if we are to get out of this mess alive we need to get that file back to ATU."

"Why would he tell you that Susan?"

"Because he wanted me to persuade you to steal it, that's why we were allowed to leave. MI5 want to force the Prime Minister to have another referendum on leaving the EU; only this time they want the right result. That's where you come in. How you get into the storage facility in the basement is up to you."

"And you agreed to this?! Fuck sake, Susan! And if we're caught?"

"We're on our own…I thought we could just disappear when we got out, I guess now that's not an option?" Silence separated them once again. "I was going to tell you," she said apologetically.

Brannigan sighed. "Matt Jones mentioned an MI5 Mole, guess he didn't get them all. Millar was sent to kill us, ATU want us alive so they killed her."

"Which means?" Said Susan,
"Which means," said Brannigan, "It would seem we have a guardian angel."

Thomas House is an imposing seven-storey building in the Pimlico district of London occupying a prime corner site on Ecclestone Square. It currently offers serviced offices to rent. The patrons of this beautiful old building have no idea what secrets its basement holds. Yet, gaining entry to the building was surprisingly easy.

Susan went online and booked Meeting Room Three under the name Chelsea Jagger from 4 pm to 6 pm the same day. According to the online brochure, this was one of the smallest rooms in the building. It was furnished only by a small round table, two chairs, a plasma screen, and a sideboard holding a jug of water and two glasses. Susan requested a laptop and printer which could be provided at no extra charge. Not that Brannigan and Blakeshaw intended to hold a meeting. Meeting room Three was beside the elevator that led to the basement and the MI5 storage facility. With the room booked, Brannigan got up to leave, "I'll meet you at Thomas House at 4 pm."

"Wait! What do you mean meet me at 4! Where are you going?"

"Got to see a man about a key. Stay here for a bit after I leave, and remember what I told you about moving round London unnoticed. Oh, and I need you to go on another tour!"

Back in her Director's Office Amelia Gallagher was busy at her desk when Matt Jones entered.

"Did you get through to Commander Chance?"

"Yes Ma'am." Well? What did he say about Agent Millar?"

"Well, he…ah…shot her, she's dead."

"What the fuck!"

"I think she must have acted with intent and Commander Chance shot her, as per your instructions Ma'am."

"I didn't tell him to kill an MI5 agent, Jesus Christ! They'll be fucking furious! We can kiss goodbye to any cooperation for about a hundred years. Unless…. we tell them that Jim Brannigan did it."

"You can't do that!" roared Matt Jones. "They'll throw everything at him. You may as well kill them both yourself! I hate Jim Brannigan as much as the next man but killing Blakeshaw is wrong. This is a pile of shit and I want no part of it!"

"You'll do as your damn well told!" shouted Amelia Gallagher. "It was your fault Sir Alistair McIntyre was killed. You didn't, or couldn't, deal with Jim Brannigan then. You're lucky you still have a job and if you fuck this up you're finished, do you hear? Besides, you're nothing more than an errand boy. So get me Julia Martin at MI5, tell her we need to talk and tell her the same place as usual. Now get out."

"You want Julia Martin, get her yourself. As I said, I want no part of this." Matt Jones stormed out of the Director's office, past Alisha Porter, and marched down the corridor to he-didn't-know-where.

Julia Martin was head of the MI5 Investigations Branch. She was tall, mid-fifties, overweight, and not well-liked. She was also nobody's fool and good at her job.

"What's this about Amelia? I'm pretty busy, one of our agents is missing and we're worried." Julia Martin was swathed in an enormous white towelling gown, lying on a gurney with a protein pack over her face and a wafer-thin cucumber slice over each eye.

Amelia Gallagher had joined her at her club, she thought Julia Martin didn't look too worried. "Look, Julia, we know you put a tail on Brannigan and Blakeshaw. The thing is Agent Millar is dead, Jim Brannigan spotted her and killed her."

Julia Martin didn't move. "And where is Jim Brannigan now?" she asked.

"Escaped with Blakeshaw" replied Gallagher.

"And Agent Millar?"

"We had no option but to lift her, she's at the ATU Morgue." Amelia Gallagher hoped that Julia Martin wouldn't want to see the body, but she was about to be disappointed.

"I want the body sent over to our pathologist Amelia and I want it understood that we will pursue Messer's Brannigan and Blakeshaw with extreme prejudice."

"Understood," replied Amelia Gallagher.

They were interrupted by the sound of the treatment room door opening.

"Well ladies I hope you're enjoying yourselves this afternoon; should I send in the masseuse?"

"Yes please" replied Julia Martin.

## Chapter Nineteen

Stonewall Security is one of the biggest security firms operating in London today. With so many staff covering so many buildings from tourist sites to hotels and more, it was easy for Susan to pick up one of their jackets as she passed through Madame Tussauds on the 2 O'clock tour.

Meanwhile, Jim Brannigan stopped on his way to Pimlico to pick up something of his own; an electronic master key from a little office supply shop on Clennan Street SE1. *Charles J Gibson and Son* had been on this street since Charlie Gibson quit the spy business in 1963 after his wife Mary gave birth to their first and only child, Noel. She figured selling paper clips was a safer occupation for a new father than spying. Except Charlie Gibson never really quit the spy business; instead he developed a nice side-line in electronic surveillance and hacking equipment. He sometimes wondered if Mary had ever questioned the fact that their rather comfortable lifestyle was based solely on the sale of paperclips. He suspected not, but they never talked about it in any case.

"Afternoon Charlie," said Brannigan as the bell above the door chimed in his arrival.

"Blow me! Jim Brannigan, as I live and breathe!" Charlie Gibson was almost seventy years of age but still looked trim and agile for a man twenty years younger.

"This place hasn't changed a bit." said Brannigan.

"Don't know about that, times change Jim, everything I sell you can now buy on the internet. I make more money selling stationery to the law offices around here than anything else. Still, with Mary passing, I've nothing else to do... Anyway, what's all this bollocks about you being a terrorist?"

"It's just that Charlie, bollocks. Listen, I don't have long here. I need an electronic master key and two of the best frequency jammers you've got."

"Is the lock industrial or private?" asked Charlie. "Definitely industrial," replied Brannigan. Charlie rummaged around in a drawer behind the counter before pulling out a master key.

"You just keep it in a drawer; don't you have a secret compartment in the wall or something?"

Charlie couldn't tell if he was being serious. "Jim, you can pick these up online for a hundred quid, but this is the best one on the market. It will check 120 codes per second, but it'll still take a good eight or nine minutes to crack a really good lock." Brannigan looked disappointed.

"This isn't the movies Jimbo, these things take time. Now, are the jammers for UHF or VHF?" He stared at Brannigan hoping for an answer; Brannigan stared back blankly. "Right then…... Multi-frequency it is."

Charlie stepped into the back of his shop and reappeared a few seconds later with two tiny black boxes. Each about the size of a cigarette lighter with three little aerials sticking out of the top. "These will jam the signal of any camera within thirty meters, just peel the cover off the back and it'll stick to pretty much anything. They can be operated manually or by remote control. I only have the one fob though." He handed the packages to Brannigan. "They also freeze the last camera image, a bit like a screenshot so you can work undetected. It's great for static cameras, not so good for roving ones though, I guess you take your chance."

"I guess so." replied Brannigan.

"You know this reminds me of the time back in '62," started Charlie but Brannigan cut him short.

"Some other time Charlie Boy, gotta go. I'll square you up later, all being well."

"You take care Jim," said Charlie as the door chimed once more and Brannigan was gone.

At 4.00 pm Brannigan and Blakeshaw entered Thomas House carrying a gym bag and a booking reference. They showed their booking reference to the Security Guard behind a rather large oak desk in reception.

"What's in the bag sir?" he asked.

"Oh, just duct tape and cable ties" Joked Brannigan and they all laughed. After a few taps on a keyboard, the guard seemed satisfied.

"That all seems in order. My name is Sean and you're both very welcome this afternoon, please follow me." They were promptly escorted toward Meeting Room Three.

"First time with us here at Thomas House?" asked Sean.

"Eh, yes it is. It's quite a beautiful building I must say," replied Susan.

"Yea, it's been around a long time. Rumour has it that the basement was once used to store government secrets during World War Two."

"Is that right?" said Brannigan, feigning interest. "That's the rumour! Mind you they're closed off now, nothing down there but the rats I'll bet! Well, here we are, Meeting Room Three."

Susan entered the room first and Brannigan stepped aside to allow Sean in behind her. He placed one of the jammers on the side of the wooden door frame and followed them into the room.

"The room comes with its own laptop and printer as requested and complimentary bottled water. You can control the heating with the thermostat on the wall and I'll be on the desk till 6.00 pm. If you need me before then just use the intercom and I'll be right round. After six, I'm on roving patrol till 10 pm but will have my radio with me at all times. Security at Thomas House is very tight, VERY TIGHT INDEED" he assured them.

At 4.20 pm Brannigan had his security jacket on, master key and jammer at the ready and a lovely new Stonewall ID Badge hanging around his neck, courtesy of the online supplier *ID Warehouse,* and the laptop and printer supplied at no extra charge.

## Chapter Twenty

Agent Matt Jones sat in front of a chicken, cheese and mayo sandwich that had started to curl ever so slightly around the edges. He had big decisions to make and lunchtime was over hours ago. He knew MI5 could operate outside the rule of law, the PM had said as much back in March when yet another seemingly obscure statement was released to Parliament. This time admitting that breaking 'domestic law' was acceptable if it was in the national interest. So, MI5 would not hesitate to do whatever they had to keep this mess from the general public, stop Brexit from happening, and kill Jim Brannigan along the way. He had to decide what he was going to do about that. He also had to decide if he had a future at ATU or indeed a future at all having just stormed out of the Director's Office and refused a direct order.

"You on your own dearie?" He looked up to see Alisha Porter grinning down at him.

"In more ways than one," he mumbled in response.

"Mind if I sit?" She didn't wait for a reply, she just plopped herself down on the only other available chair. "You don't look so good, you okay dearie?"

Matt Jones did his best to ignore her.

"Still, it must be wonderful for you to work

for that lovely Ms. Gallagher? Do you know she gave me the rest of the day off, said she wouldn't be back in the office today, something about arranging a funeral."

Matt Jones jumped up, pushed his chair back, and left the chicken sandwich with Alisha Porter. He had a funeral to get to and it was already 4 O'clock.

He ran through the building and seconds later his black SUV screeched out of the car park and nearly smashed into the side of a refuge truck before swinging into Harleyford Road and onward to Waterloo. He shoved his earwig into his ear as tyres burned and horns blared.

"Commander Chance, this is Agent Jones; what's your twenty? Commander, do you copy, over?" but there was no answer from Commander Chance.

"Deputy Commander Gerrard, this is Special Agent Jones do you copy?" This time he got a reply.

"This is Deputy Commander Gerrard, over"

"I need an update on Brannigan and Blakeshaw and I want to know where Commander Chance is."

"Brannigan and Blakeshaw are in Thomas House, Pimlico. No word on Commander

Chance," came the terse reply. He wasn't going to get much out of Deputy Commander Gerrard.

"I'm on my way and will assume command when I get there, send me your location, out."

With the late afternoon traffic it would take twenty minutes or so to get to Pimlico, the problem was he didn't know what he was going to do when he got there. He had decided one thing though, letting Brannigan and Blakeshaw get killed wasn't an option.

"Jim, it's nearly time to go, air temperature in the basement is fast approaching 37 Degrees Celsius. Once it reaches body temperature the Infrared Sensors won't be able to detect you. I reckon you'll have maybe ten minutes max in that heat to get the files and get out, after that you may become disorientated and lose consciousness." Susan Blakeshaw sat at the little round table in Meeting Room Three having just hacked the Air Con system at Thomas House.

On the screen in front of her were the schematics of the building and the basement glowed red. According to the poster on the wall the Air Con was a state-of-the-art system, Wi-Fi controlled and designed *to create a flexible, sustainable, and comfortable working space for all*. It could also be used for a serious bit of breaking and entering in the right hands.

"Most likely the sensors in the cameras operate on a dual system which means they use Infrared radiation to detect body heat and microwave radiation to detect body movement but remember it takes both sensors to trigger the alarm, otherwise they get too many false positives. You should be able to move about but do it slowly and use the jammer as a backup. We'll have to take the chance they're not running on separate systems." She looked up at Brannigan.

"Susan, it's me you're talking to," He said "I know all of this shit."

"Guess I'm just nervous," she replied rather sheepishly. "Remember this though, when the elevator doors open wait until the temperature reaches 37 Degrees again before going into the basement." Brannigan remembered Charlie Gibson had also said something about taking a chance. He really would need a bit of luck on this one.

"Let's do this," he said.

He clicked the fob and the signal jammer in the corridor bleeped into life, a little green eye blinking out at the world. This would give him all the time he needed. However, the next eight minutes would feel like an eternity. At least the electronic lock for the elevator looked like it was of standard design, which meant that it was easy to break into. It was made up of three distinct parts, the outer part which consisted solely of the touch screen keypad for entering the pin number, the inner part which is the connector or conduit that links the keypad to the third part, the lock itself. The casing on this type of lock is not alarmed; there is no protection for the keypad, it is assumed that the cameras and the security guards provide that protection. The lock will shut down and send out a distress signal if three unsuccessful attempts are made to input the pin number but with the master key that wasn't a concern of his.

    Brannigan jimmied the screen off with his penknife to expose the internal connector. This part of the lock has no way of checking what exactly it's connected to, so he unplugged the screen and connected his master key instead. Then he waited for his device to crack the pin code and call the elevator from the basement. Time wore on and eight minutes turned into ten while Brannigan stood anxiously by.

    He had no patience for waiting around like this because he knew how dangerous it could be. Frustration boiled inside him and he kicked the shit out of the lock with the heel of his boot. Sparks flew and circuit boards exploded, then he grabbed a couple of wires and shoved them together because most of all he wanted to see those fucking elevator doors open! Except he knew if he did that he'd just end up with a busted lock and a sore foot, so he waited. He checked his watch again; this was taking way too long. Still, he had enough time if everything else went according to plan....

The sound of footsteps, soft on the carpet, and the gentle crackle of a radio receiver alerted him to the oncoming danger and he stood in front of the keypad, keeping his back tight against the wall effectively blocking it from view. He figured the jacket and ID badge would be enough to keep away any unwanted attention. Unfortunately for him, it was a security guard with gold epaulettes that walked around the corner. A look of surprise flashed across his face when he saw Brannigan practically standing to attention beside the elevator.

"What are you doing here?" he asked "There's no security detail scheduled for this corridor today."

Brannigan shrugged his shoulders, "Front desk sent me, told me to wait by the elevator for further instructions."

"I'm the Daytime Shift Leader, nobody told me about this. What's your name?"

Brannigan hadn't time to answer; the ping

from the master key and the noise of the elevator rising from the basement startled them both.

"What's going here!" demanded the guard and he reached for Brannigan's ID badge.

That was all the movement Jim Brannigan needed. He grabbed the man's forearm and spun him around. Standing behind him now he wrapped his right arm tightly around the man's neck under his jaw and he squeezed upwards. With his left hand, he pushed the back of the man's head forward into the headlock. The guard struggled at first, grabbing frantically at Brannigan's arm in a vain attempt to flee. His feet slid on the carpet as he flailed about, desperately trying to get enough traction to run or push back against his assailant. But in the end, all he could do was rasp out a cry for help as the pressure increased and his eyes widened at the realisation that he was going to die.

Except, like our Glaswegian friend on the bus, Jim Brannigan had no intention of killing this innocent man. All he was doing was applying sufficient pressure on the vagus nerve in the neck to induce a faint, and sure enough the security guard with the gold epaulettes passed out and collapsed into Brannigan's arms. He dragged the guard into Meeting Room Three and with the help of a rather startled-looking Susan gagged and bound him using duct tape and cable ties.

"How long will he be out?" asked Susan.

"Couple of minutes, max," replied Brannigan.

"Couple of minutes!" cried, Susan.

"It's not like the movies Susan." Brannigan took the guard's radio and after a quick search, he took his wallet and mobile phone. The driver's licence told him the guard with the gold epaulettes was one Timothy Jamison, 23, from Oldham Street, London SE2.

Brannigan removed the master key, clipped the screen back on and entered the waiting elevator to descend to the basement. He checked his watch and at 4.32 pm the elevator doors opened into the basement. He was greeted by a wall of heat. It took a few seconds for the Air Con system to quietly buzz into action and then stop again moments later. He reached out of the elevator and stuck the second jammer onto the wall. Another click of the fob blinked it into existence. The basement was stifling hot.

Every breath burned its way into his lungs causing his airway to contract and his throat to close, making it difficult to breathe. Deep breaths were impossible while short, shallow breaths left him feeling lightheaded. There was simply not enough oxygen getting into his body.

He was so focused on breathing that he struggled to gather his thoughts. He'd be lucky to last ten minutes at this rate.

The basement was filled with row upon row of metal storage units stretching from floor to ceiling. In a bizarre almost hallucinating way they reminded him of an IKEA store, all conveniently labelled for easy shopping. In this case by year from left to right starting with 1946 and then sorted alphabetically down each row with little flags for each letter of the alphabet clearly visible. He was looking for 2018, section C which he found easily enough for someone who felt like a drunken man stumbling about in the dark.

Each section was further divided into subsections and he found subsection J. Sure enough, there was the Carter File still wrapped in its little plastic folder with Alex's USB stick inside. Brannigan took the file. It was all he could do now to put one foot in front of the other. He pushed the elevator button for the ground floor and the promise of fresh air.

It was a welcome relief when the doors opened. He closed his eyes as his nostrils flared and his lungs drank in the colder air. The rush of oxygen caused him to feel giddy and he steadied himself against the wall of the elevator.

Just a Daytime Shift Leader to worry about, then they would be home free.

Susan sat at the little round table with the Daytime Shift Leader motionless at her feet. Brannigan entered the meeting room and nodded in his direction.

"Right, You, up!" and he kicked the guard's foot.

"He's still unconscious Jim! He hasn't moved since you left" said Susan, sounding a little alarmed that he was kicking an unconscious man.

"Not a chance." replied Brannigan and he kicked the guard's foot again, "Next time I'll put a bullet in it."

"Okay, Okay," mumbled the security guard through the gag. He scrambled up onto his knees and Brannigan helped him into the other chair.

"My friend here wants me to kill you." He gestured toward Susan with a flick of his thumb, "Says it'll be easier that way. Says you'll talk if we let you live." Brannigan looked over to Susan and back to the security guard and removed his gag "What do you say……….. Timothy?"

The guard's eyes widened at the mention of his name. "Please, please let me live, I won't tell anyone…. Honest." pleaded the guard..

"Well Timothy, I don't think that's necessarily

true but I'll tell you something. We've just stolen a secret government file from right under your nose and everyone connected to this file has been killed. You may have seen the news about the terrorist attacks in Edinburgh and London this week and the one about that poor Russian girl killed on a night out with pals. All of it is lies Timothy, all of these people knew about this file and now they're dead and now you know about the file too."

Brannigan used his penknife and cut the cable ties. "Here's the thing. If you tell anyone about what we just did then you're putting yourself and your family in danger. You'll most definitely die in some tragic accident and you might get them killed as well. So, it's up to you. Let us walk out of here and you live or raise the alarm, in which case we'll probably escape anyway and you'll die at the hands of the government agents they will send after you……. or I'll come back and kill you myself. After all, I know where you live." He flashed the driver's licence at Timothy.

He turned to Susan, "Let's go," and with that, they left Daytime Shift Leader Timothy Jamison in Meeting Room Three along with an extra ID Badge and Jacket. They passed Sean behind his big desk, giving him and wave and a smile and at 4.55 pm they were standing on the steps of Thomas House looking for somewhere to plan the next move, and maybe get a much-needed coffee before heading to Pimlico Tube Station and onward to a rendezvous at ATU.

## Chapter Twenty One

"Yes Ma'am, I'm sure…Someone triggered the *Fool Catcher* in Thomas House at 4.32 pm today…*The Fool Catcher* Ma'am, it's the name we give to a backup device that catches people out because they're not expecting it…In this case, it's a Volumetric Air Pressure Sensor Ma'am…It detects movement by calculating variations in air pressure, but it needs another sensor to trigger an alarm…It sends an alert to HQ for investigation…No, they weren't picked up on CCTV and no alarm sounded…... Our cameras picked up two people leaving Thomas House at 4.55 pm…. Yes, they have been identified as Jim Brannigan and Susan Blakeshaw…Yes Ma'am, right away."

Jo Beresford hung up the phone and sighed. She had been working for MI5 Investigations Branch for over a year, but she still felt stressed when talking to the Head of Investigations, Julia Martin. Even though she was sitting in a room on the other side of London she felt as though Julia Martin could see her every move and that freaked her out. In truth, she wasn't wrong.

On the other side of London Julia Martin was deep in conversation. "Well Amelia, you heard what Ms. Beresford had to say. They've stolen the file and I want it back. And I want

Brannigan dead. You agreed, and I don't care what anybody thinks. We'll get the file, you take care of Brannigan and Blakeshaw, this is your mess so clean it up."

Damn if she was going to be denied revenge for the death of one of her agents, even if she couldn't remember the poor girl's name, and the file was key to keeping the United Kingdom in the EU. The PM would do as they're told once MI5 had the file back for leverage, the Home Secretary would see to that.

"Well, not *my* mess exactly but like I said, we'll take care of it. Trust me." replied Amelia Gallagher. But Julia Martin didn't trust Amelia Gallagher. She suspected that maybe she was starting to think she actually was the new Director of ATU. It looked like removing Jim Brannigan from the face of this Earth would be a matter for MI5.

"Okay Amelia, good. I'm glad we cleared that up. I'll send a squad over to Pimlico to intercept Messers Brannigan and Blakeshaw. Once I have the file I'll leave the rest to you."

"Why don't you just wait until I have the file, then I'll give it to you?" asked Gallagher.

"Because, dear Amelia, ATU cannot be trusted. You've already killed two previous Directors over this file and frankly, I've no confidence you won't be next" Julia Martin gazed, wide-eyed at Amelia Gallagher. Amelia Gallagher got the impression she was being dismissed.

"I'll speak to Commander Chance and sort things my end." And with that, she left Julia Martin to her thoughts.

Jo Beresford's intercom buzzed," Get me Sam Evans," ordered Julia Martin.

While Julia Martin was awaiting the arrival of Sam Evans, Amelia Gallagher contacted Commander Chance with some specific instructions of her own.

"Commander I want you to proceed to Pimlico, liaise with your surveillance teams, and shadow Brannigan and Blakeshaw. Once MI5 has the file you are green light to execute the assets."

"Say again" replied Commander Chance,
"You heard, Gallagher out."

It was 6.00 pm on a beautiful Thursday evening in London and Amelia Gallagher decided to take a stroll along the Thames. It would all be over soon and then she could go back to GCHQ and her role as an MI5 agent.

Jo Beresford had contacted Sam Evans as instructed. He waited until Amelia Gallagher left the building before entering Julia Martin's office.

"Sam this is straightforward; I want the file and I want this situation tidied up once and for all. I don't want Brannigan and Blakeshaw to pop up anywhere but in one of our morgues. Do you understand?"

"Absolutely Ma'am, my team is following the targets and will intercept on my command. What about ATU?"

"Don't worry about ATU, I've taken care of that. Just get the file and kill them both"

"Ma'am"

Sam Evans left Thames House too but headed away from the river and onward to Pimlico and an unscheduled appointment with death.

They entered *Tom Tom's Café* in Chester Street in West London and Brannigan smiled at the nice lady behind the counter. A quick glance at her badge confirmed her name as Lucy. "Two coffees please, Lucy"

"Sorry, I'm just about to close."

"We really could use a couple of coffees."

"Well, you both do look as if you've had a rough day. What type of coffee would you like? We've got cappuccino, latte, flat white, regular white or regular black."

"Two regular black coffees will be fine" replied Brannigan. He sat facing Susan, cradling a cup in his hands. The steam from the hot liquid tickled his nose. "So, what's the plan?" he said sipping his drink.

"We're to get ourselves over to the London Eye, we'll be intercepted on the way and we are to hand over the file. Then we're free to go." replied Susan.

"And who will we be handing the file to?" enquired Brannigan. "Matt Jones" replied Susan.

"Great" was the terse reply. The coffee was good and the semblance of normality it gave was welcome.

Assistant Commander Brendan Gerrard sat in the front passenger seat of one of the new Guardian Response Vehicles, a Junker-built armoured car purchased by the Government to combat the terrorist threat in London and deployed in recent months around the city of Westminster. This GRV was parked just off Morton Street in the Pimlico district of London and Assistant Commander Gerrard was trying his best to take no notice of Special Agent Matt Jones who was sulking in the back of the vehicle, squashed between two members of the ATU Special Forces Unit.

He had turned up as he had promised and attempted to take charge, but Brendan Gerrard only had one boss and until Commander Chance arrived he was the one in charge, not Special Agent Jones. He was however happy to provide Matt Jones with an update. Brannigan and Blakeshaw had entered Thomas House at 4.00 pm and since then nothing had happened. The back doors of the vehicle cranked open and Matt Jones let out an audible sigh at the sight of Commander Chance.

"Well, well, well Special Agent Jones......how's your day been going so far?"

"Downhill now you're here" huffed Matt Jones.

Brendan Gerrard interrupted, "Sir, Brannigan, and Blakeshaw have just left Thomas House, the mobile crew is following as per your instructions." He pressed the earpiece tight against his ear, "...Looks like they've picked up a shadow team. There's at least one, two-man team following from about 50 yards."

"They've got to be MI5," said Matt Jones. He looked up at Commander Chance, "You know she told MI5 that Brannigan killed Sharon Millar? Said she didn't want to upset *relations* between ATU and MI5 by telling them the truth, said she was going to let MI5 kill them both in any case."

Brendan Gerrard interrupted for a second time, "Sir, mobile crew report Brannigan and Blakeshaw entering Tom Tom's Coffee House on Chester Street."

Commander Chance nodded in acknowledgment while still listening to Matt Jones. "I've arranged to intercept them on their way to the London Eye then they're free to go. That was the deal I made with Susan Blakeshaw. I'm just about to head off there now."

"Well you're not in charge, Amelia Gallagher is, and it seems, she wants them dead...... one way or another," replied Adam Chance.

Brannigan and Blakeshaw sat at the back of the little cafe longer than they should have. Eventually leaving around 5.30 pm as Lucy with the nice smile really wanted to close up for the day. They almost collided with a jogger who stopped just ahead of them. Panting for breath, bent over, hands resting on his knees but there was no sweat on his brow and there was the unmistakable bulge of a shoulder holster under his sweat top.

Brannigan reached into his jacket and unclipped his Glock. The action was noted by the jogger. "Whoa! I'm only here to collect the file, nothing else," Sam Evans raised his arms in mock surrender. "You give me the file and you're free to go" his smile was weak.

"Where's Matt Jones?" asked Susan

"Don't know, off sick today I think. All I

know is they sent me instead. Now hand over the file," demanded Sam Evans, all pretence of friendliness suddenly gone.

"No problem, here you go," said Brannigan. "Glad to get rid of it, to be honest" He held out the file and as Agent Evans reached for it he let it slip out of his fingers. Evans instinctively went to grab it and Brannigan stuck the muzzle of his Glock into his rib cage and dragged him back into the coffee shop. Susan picked up the file and followed them. Lucy was frozen to the spot when she saw the Glock. "No need to worry love, honestly." assured Brannigan.

Brendan Gerrard interrupted for a third time, his finger still pressing hard on the earwig in his ear. "Sir, shots fired at the Café, Brannigan, and Blakeshaw inside with an unidentified male."

"For Christ's sake Chance do something, they're going to get killed!" shouted Matt Jones but Adam Chance did nothing.

"Fuck this!" Matt Jones burst out of the back doors of the armoured car and ran toward Chester Street and Tom Tom's café.

The windows of the little café exploded under a hail of bullets and Lucy with the nice smile died.

"Out the back!" shouted Brannigan. Susan was already on the floor and scrambled on her hands and knees across splintered glass and wood toward the counter and out through the back of the shop. Brannigan was still holding on to Agent Evans, but he was beyond help. His grey sweat suit stained red, his body lifeless.

The shooting stopped almost as quickly as it had begun. He let Sam Evans slip from his arms and ran toward the back of the shop. Shiny slithers of glass mixed with blood twinkled on Susan's hands and knees but there was no time to stop. Agents poured into *Tom Tom's* as Brannigan and Blakeshaw raced down the back alleyway, with MI5 in hot pursuit. They practically skidded around the corner and almost smashed straight into Special Agent Jones. His gun was drawn and Brannigan had no time to react as Matt Jones raised the weapon and fired… killing the MI5 agent over Brannigan's left shoulder.

"Let's get the fuck out of here!" Brannigan and Blakeshaw didn't have to be told twice.

The three of them bolted out onto Chiswick Street; Matt Jones in Front, Brannigan at the rear. They surged through the crowd, pushing, shoving, and shouting their way to God knows where. MI5 were moving fast in behind them but soon they'd be in front of them and to the side of them and then they'd be trapped.

"In Here!" yelled Matt Jones flicking his head back at Susan before ducking through the gates of St Saviour's Church. He bounded up the steps to the huge wooden doors and pulled the handle in a mixture of relief and desperation, he reckoned even MI5 wouldn't storm a church. He was to be disappointed however because the doors of St Saviours' were locked, "Fuck!" he exclaimed as Brannigan and Blakeshaw practically ran over the top of him.

"You're a dick." was all Brannigan could say before bullets whizzed past, peppering the front of St Saviours'. Brannigan spun around, dropped low and fired off a couple of shots at the agents spewing into the church grounds. "Round the back!" he shouted.

They ran fast and hard but not fast enough; a bullet from a Sig P226 caught Matt Jones square in the back. He shot forward, stumbled, and collapsed in the graveyard. Brannigan dragged him behind a large tomb belonging to someone called Sir John Lubick. The lock to Sir John's final resting place gave way under pressure from Brannigan's boot and Susan helped him drag the injured agent inside.

He grabbed Matt Jones' earpiece, "Agent down, I repeat agent down. Urgent assistance needed to St Saviour's Church, Pimlico". Instinctively, they moved to the back of the Tomb and waited but there was no response from ATU.

"Sir, Shadow Team have entered the café...... now in pursuit of Brannigan, Blakeshaw. Special Agent Jones has arrived and has exchanged gunfire with MI5...... they're running down St George's Avenue......they've entered St Saviours Church. Shots fired."

Brendan Gerrard glared at Commander Chance, "I repeat shots fired!" he shouted. "What do we do Sir?"

"Our job," came the curt reply. Seconds passed, and time slowed.

All comms crackled, "Agent down, I repeat agent down. Urgent assistance needed to St Saviour's Church, Pimlico." Gerrard was staring at Chance, willing him to send help, willing him to do something, but Chance stood silent. He didn't owe Jim Brannigan anything.

"No one's coming" whispered Brannigan in desperation. Silence filled the graveyard as agents took up their positions outside. The only noise came from the hum of traffic and the wail of distant sirens. "I'm sorry Susan", he continued "I'm sorry for dragging you into this.

I'm sorry for Jennifer. I'm sorry for everything." His voice crackled, and his throat was dry, the sort of dryness that only comes from fear. For the first time in his life, he was all out of ideas and he was afraid, here, at the end.

"Some fucking agent you are." mumbled Matt Jones. "Give me the earpiece."

"This is Special Agent Matt Jones. I need urgent medical assistance. I repeat I need urgent medical assistance."

The seconds ground on and still there was no response from ATU.

"Adam, I'm in trouble," and with that, Matt Jones died.

## Chapter Twenty Two

Commander Chance looked over at Brendan Gerrard. "Well, what the fuck are we waiting for!" He slammed the back doors shut and the vehicle roared into life.

ATU Special Forces thundered along St George's Avenue and swung sharp right, blocking the street to face St Saviour's Church. Seven tonnes of armour rumbled up the kerb and bull-bars cracked their way through seventeenth-century stone. People panicked and ran in fear, others stood with mobile phones in outstretched arms.

The distinctive high-pitched whirring of the vehicle was drawing attention from inside the church grounds too. It must have been quite a terrifying sight for an MI5 agent setting siege because, orders or not, Shadow Team turned tail and scarpered as this monster on wheels crunched its way into the graveyard and ATU Special Forces sprang from the belly of the beast.

"In here!" shouted Brannigan.

ATU swept through the graveyard while Commander Chance ran low and hard, covering the ground between the GRV and the final resting place of Sir John Lubick in seconds. At the back of the tomb he found Matt Jones. He stared at the dead agent and then looked up at

Brannigan and Blakeshaw. "Let's get you two out of here" was all he said.

Back in the Guardian they were prisoners of their own silence, wrapped in thought and grief but something else stirred in Commander Chance…

*"In other news, police are advising motorists to expect delays in and around St George's Avenue after an unidentified woman was shot dead by armed assailants at Tom Tom's Coffee House in the area in a suspected robbery gone wrong. Police have said that one of the attackers was shot at the scene while others escaped down a back alleyway. The condition of the attacker is not known, and no other details are available at this time. The victim's relatives have been informed and police are not treating the shooting as a terrorist attack. In an unrelated incident, a stolen car crashed into St Saviour's Church today causing substantial damage to the front door of the 17th Century building and the adjacent graveyard. Police are appealing for witnesses."*

"Turn that shit off" said a voice from the back. Silence captured them once more.

The Guardian's V8 engines powered down as it slowed to turn right into a grey building in Vauxhall Cross. No one took any notice of the unmarked van parked down the side street opposite with its roller door wide open. If they had, they would have seen a man standing up in the back of the van. But more than that, he was strapped into the van, part of the van almost, like a spider in the centre of a web. A web of steel and rubber with this man being held in the middle with only his arms free and in them he held the RGP7 portable, anti-tank, rocket launcher. As the back of the Guardian came into his line of sight he placed the rocket launcher on his left shoulder, aimed the weapon at the underside of the vehicle and pulled the launching trigger activating the rocket propulsion system. The grenade flew out of the barrel, the man recoiled into his rubber web and the van sped away as the roller doors closed.

Being inside an armoured car under rocket attack is a terrifying experience and, in truth, few survive the ordeal. The grenade exploded and the vehicle shot forward, tumbling through the air. Inside bodies smashed into flesh and metal. Heads cracked open, blurred faces flashed past one another. There was screaming, shouting and squealing. An eye socket exploded and bones snapped. Smoke and heat stole the air from their lungs and death arrived.

Passers-by rushed in to rip open doors and drag out the injured and dying from the upturned husk of the vehicle. Sirens shrieked in the distance and more help would arrive, but most were beyond help.

Jim Brannigan looked around at the devastation. His body was wrecked with pain; his jaw was broken, his left hand smashed to pieces, and his lungs filled with blood. In the developing horror of recognition for one he cared for, he fell to his knees and wailed. The kind of guttural howl that only an animal in pain and beyond the edge of despair can make. Bawling his last breath into a world that doesn't care, he screamed
"Susan!"

## Epilogue

In the weeks and months that followed the incident at Vauxhall Cross Brexit negotiations between the United Kingdom and the European Union were played out in the public arena. Senior politicians squabbled and bickered as only senior politicians can. The Foreign Secretary resigned, and the Prime Minister appeared to be in turmoil. A deal with the EU seemed simultaneously within reach and as far away as ever.

The real driver behind these scenes of silliness however was the power struggle between the British Security Services for the future of the United Kingdom, each one wanting to push their agenda to the fore.

Meanwhile, Adam Chance left the ATU once discharged from the hospital. He had broken nearly every bone in his body and lost sight in one eye and he walked with the aid of a stick. He intended to retire to somewhere warm, but first, he had something to do for an old friend......

The day he left the hospital his mobile rang. "You ready to do this?" said the voice on the other end of the phone.

"Absolutely" replied Adam Chance

Amelia Gallagher was found hanged off London Bridge one cold winter morning.

It was reported that the young social worker had suffered from depression in the weeks before her death. Nothing more than another sad statistic to blight the city.

Julia Martin accidently drowned in her bath at home after taking a cocktail of prescription drugs and alcohol. The Coroner recorded a verdict of misadventure. She had no known relatives.

Police records show that Jim Brannigan died at the scene of an explosion in Vauxhall Cross. He was a known terrorist and it was suspected that he blew himself up while in the process of planting the device.

Printed by Amazon Italia Logistica S.r.l.
Torrazza Piemonte (TO), Italy